Society Ciphers

A NOVEL

By Fernando Jose Araujo

SOCIETY CIPHERS
By: Fernando Jose Araujo

ISBN – 9798218312534

Summary

When the mayor of Minneapolis is suddenly abducted, the
Chief of Police, James Willie, seeks help from Consulting
Detective Connor and his partner Jim. As the two detectives
search for the mayor, they find themselves in a rabbit hole of
a mysterious serial killer, human trafficking, and a
frightening conspiracy.

Table of Contents

Prologue
The Mayor's Speech

"People of Minneapolis, it has come to my attention that our city has been overrun by crime over the past few years. But fear not, for I will be working with our chief of police, James Willie, to clean up our city. With the state's approval, we can now expect the city's taxes to increase. This, in turn, is essential if we intend to proceed with our plan," Mayor Johnson announced in front of a large crowd of reporters.

As soon as Mayor Johnson made his announcement, reporters flooded him with questions. Having to hear the reporters' questions, he felt lightheaded watching them struggle. He tried to decide who to answer first, but he couldn't make up his mind and listened instead.

"Mayor Johnson, have you considered the negative effects a tax increase could have on the city?" one of the several reporters shouted out from the crowd.

"Mayor Johnson, don't you think it would be better to instead invest the money from the taxes in the city's economy? Rather than paying extra to the city's officers?" another one of the several reporters shouted out.

Before Mayor Johnson could respond to the many reporters' questions, his bodyguards escorted him. Fleeing the press, he'd later be faced with more questions. However, he rolled his eyes and kept on walking away. As he was about to enter his limousine, a journalist suddenly shouted.

"Mayor Johnson! Please, I just have *one* question I need to ask you."

During a brief pause in his walk, Mayor Johnson glanced back at the journalist. Clenching his jaw, Mayor Johnson sighed and nodded at the journalist. Before speaking into her microphone, the journalist cleared her throat.

"In recent months, numerous government officials in Des Moines and Omaha have been murdered. Both are highly populated cities of the two states, Iowa and Nebraska. There have also been rumors of an alleged serial killer who has been behind these murders and many more. Media outlets have dubbed the killer as *The Mortem*. Another odd thing about this murderer is that they specifically target government officials. So, my question to you is, are you worried you may also be targeted by The Mortem?" the journalist said, placing her microphone near Mayor Johnson.

"… No comment," Mayor Johnson said, entering his limousine.

While sitting inside his limousine, Mayor Johnson watched protesters gather outside City Hall. Among the signs held up by protesters were those calling for his impeachment. They also had signs stating that the government was evil. Shrugging his shoulders, he looked at the mini fridge inside his limousine. Opening the mini fridge, he took out a bottle of wine and poured himself a drink.

Arriving at his apartment building, Mayor Johnson's bodyguards escorted him to his penthouse. Walking through the hallway leading to his penthouse, his bodyguards followed behind. Entering his penthouse, his wife Martha greeted him with a kiss.

"I've missed you," Martha said, smooching Mayor Johnson.

"Have you now? How's Amelia? Is she asleep?" Mayor Johnson asked.

"Yes, I tucked her in just now. Anyway, how was the speech to the press?"

"Well, besides being asked a ton of irritating questions. It went rather well… But there was this one journalist who asked a rather unnerving question."

"Really? What did they ask you?"

"… You know what? It doesn't matter, because all I want to do now is sit back and relax," Mayor Johnson said, as he sat on a sofa and turned on the television.

Hours later, still sitting on the sofa chair, Mayor Johnson began to drift off. Gradually falling asleep, he suddenly heard a noise come from the kitchen. His eyes widened while a sense of dread swept through his mind. His heart began pounding when he heard footsteps coming from the kitchen.

But Mayor Johnson's heart soon relaxed once he saw it was Amelia. Amelia had a glass of water in her hand and smiled at him. Realizing it was nothing for him to worry about, he chuckled.

"Daddy, are you okay?" Amelia asked.

"I am, my dear. I'm just a bit tired… Anyway, let's get you back to bed," Mayor Johnson said, walking Amelia to her room.

Tucking Amelia into bed, Mayor Johnson gave her a good night kiss, but just when he was about to leave, Amelia shouted, "Wait, you forgot something!"

Rubbing his chin, he looked around until he realized he had forgotten to turn on her nightlight. When he eventually turned on her night light, Amelia giggled while she held onto her teddy bear. Mayor Johnson smiled as he went up to Amelia and patted her head.

"Thank you, Daddy, I love you," Amelia said, smiling.

"I love you too, sweetie. Now, go to bed. It's already past your bedtime," Mayor Johnson said, leaving Amelia's room.

Stepping out of Amelia's room, he suddenly received a phone call. However, as soon as he saw the caller's name, his eyes widened. Answering the phone, he took a deep breath before speaking.

"Hello sir, is something wrong? Why are you calling me so late?"

"Nothing is wrong in particular… But there has been a *dispute* with our business partner. You do know who I'm talking about right?" the caller said.

"Of course, I know who… But what do you suggest I do?"

"Oh, you don't have to worry about that, it is being handled. But I do have a new assignment for you. So, since you'll be increasing the city's taxes, we now have an opportunity to work with a new business partner… Therefore, I would like you to find us someone, someone who will not try to oppose us. Otherwise, we will have to make an example of them… like our prior business partner."

As Mayor Johnson contemplated the request, he suddenly felt a cold sensation on his feet. Looking down to see what caused the feeling, his jaw dropped as he saw a puddle of blood soaking his feet. Following the blood, a chill ran down his spine when he saw it coming from the master bedroom.

When Mayor Johnson glanced into the bedroom, his heart stopped. He couldn't believe his eyes when he found the dead body of his wife. Due to the shock, he lost grip of his phone, causing it to fall on the floor.

Now slowly moving toward his wife, he witnessed her inside a pool of blood. In tears, he fell to his knees and held on to her, sobbing. However, in doing so, he noticed that the nose and eyes of her face were missing, as if someone had cut them off.

Following that, he suddenly heard someone whistling nearby. However, before he left the bedroom, he opened a nearby cabinet drawer. Opening the cabinet, he took out a pistol and loaded a magazine into it. With every second feeling like a decade, his breathing grew heavier as he pursued the whistling around his penthouse.

Now in the living room, he aimed his pistol frantically, not knowing where the intruder could be. Hearing someone suddenly snap their fingers, he gasped. Turning to see who snapped their fingers, he found a hooded man sitting on his sofa chair. Aside from the leather hooded jacket, the hooded man wore a full-face helmet and some kind of body armor.

"… Who are you? Why did you kill my wife!" Mayor Johnson shouted, aiming his pistol at the hooded man.

Without saying a word, the hooded man threw something at Mayor Johnson, which landed on the floor. Glancing at what the hooded man tossed, Mayor Johnson became nauseous when he realized that the hooded man threw his wife's nose and eyes.

Taking out a baseball bat, the hooded man then gradually stood up from the sofa chair. Seeing this, Mayor Johnson snapped and started shooting frantically at the hooded man. Unfazed by the multiple bullets fired at him, the hooded man persisted.

Having run out of ammunition, Mayor Johnson became defenseless. Before he could act, the hooded man struck his head with the baseball, causing the mayor to plummet to the floor. Having been nearly knocked unconscious, he tried to stand back up. However, the hooded man grabbed onto his head and smashed it on the floor several times.

After being beaten by the hooded man, all Mayor Johnson could do was watch what the hooded man was about to do next. Gazing at the hooded man, he saw the hooded man take out a large garbage bag and syringe from his garment bag. Realizing what the hooded man was planning, he decided to try and crawl away. However, it would be futile as the hooded man dragged him back and proceeded to inject him with the syringe. Once injected, he soon felt the effects consuming him. Though, as he was blacking out, the last thing he saw was Amelia, watching from afar in the hallway, sobbing.

"… Why are you doing this? What have we ever done to you?" Mayor Johnson mumbled, blacking out.

Chapter 1
The Case of Billy

Around noon, Connor and Jim linger in their black car, where they stalk a nearby house. Waiting for one of the residents to leave the house, Jim used binoculars to see the house from a distance. Connor, meanwhile, examined a case file with Billy Carter's missing person poster.

When going over Billy's poster, Connor turned to look at Jim, and asked, "So, you think we have the right house?"

"Well, based on what most of the neighbors told us, there have been sightings of Billy inside the house. There was also a report from a neighbor who saw Billy thrown into the back trunk of one of the residents' cars. My biggest concern however is that a lot of the neighbors have mentioned some unusual behavior from the residents lately. One of the neighbors even said that one night she heard some sort of prayer being chanted in the backyard of the house. When she took a closer look at the backyard. She mentioned that the residents were performing some kind of ritual while wearing black cloaks," Jim clarified, continuing to keep an eye on the house with his binoculars.

"Now that sure is concerning... Well, regardless of what these people do during their free time, we have to focus on finding that kid."

A few minutes later, Jim, still watching the house, saw an old man exit the front door. Jim watched closely as the old man got into a car and drove away. After this, Connor and Jim proceed to follow the old man, eventually following the old man to a local bar. Thinking it would be their best opportunity to question the old man, Connor was about to go inside, but had his arm tugged by Jim.

"Connor wait, let's try thinking this one over first," Jim said.

"What? What do you mean? He's right there. What's there to think about?" Connor said, raising an eyebrow.

"Look, he's drinking and by the looks of it, he's going to drink until he collapses. And based on my experience, a drunk person usually tells the truth or is more open to a conversation."

"Wait, is that actually true? Hmm, alright, I guess we'll have to wait until our pal can't drink anymore."

"Yes, but something about this old man seems familiar... Almost like I've seen him somewhere before.

After an hour, the old man finally left the bar. The old man stumbled as he walked, which led to the man collapsing on the ground. As the old man struggled to get up, he was suddenly grabbed by his shirt and pinned to a wall by Connor. This resulted in the old man screaming, but was then punched by Connor, silencing the old man.

"Easy Connor, we still don't know if he's guilty of anything yet," Jim said, placing his hand on Connor's shoulder.

"Who are you, people? Why did you hit me? Please, don't hurt me, I have money, lots of it… Just please let me go—" the old man said but got cut off by Connor.

"We don't want your money! Listen, we are consulting detectives and we're looking for this kid. Do you know where he is?" Connor said, showing the old man Billy's missing person poster.

The moment the old man laid his eyes on the poster of Billy, his eyes widened and whispered, "I knew one day, this was going to happen… Yes, I know where he is. I regret so much for partaking in what we did to that poor boy."

"What? Okay, then tell us! Where are you keeping him? Spill it, old man!" Connor shouted.

"My son, Richard… He took him to our family's cabin. I can write down the address of the cabin, but I don't know if the boy is still alive."

"Wait, Richard? As in Richard Thompson? The one who tried to run for district council four years ago but lost?" Jim asked.

"Yes, that's correct… After Richard lost the election, he had a meltdown. Occasionally, he would destroy the furniture in our house. He stayed like that for almost two weeks and one day he suddenly changed in personality. After that day, everything becomes blurry. I can't seem to remember much of what happened… But what I do remember is what we all had to do to that child," the old man said, bursting into tears.

Watching the old man fall apart in front of them, Connor knew the old man needed help. His eyebrows lowered, as he imagined if he were in the old man's place. Squatting down, he patted the old man's shoulder as he said the following.

"Alright listen, you look like you've been through a lot… I'm sorry I hit you before, but if what you're saying is true, then we'll go to this address and see if we can save this kid. However, we're going to take you to the police and you're gonna have to confess to everything that you've done… And maybe they can get you the help you need."

Upon dropping off the old man at the police station, they informed the police of the address, though they proceeded to the address first. Now, on the road, they drove along the highway that led to the address. While Jim drove, Connor contemplated what the old man told them.

Fearing they may be going the wrong way, Connor looked at Jim and asked, "Hey, you think it was a good idea for us to have trusted what an intoxicated old man would say? Like, sure drunk people usually do, tell the truth, but how true is that?"

"Well, even if he wasn't drunk when he told us his story, what other leads do we have? Almost no other residents even leave that house. And we can't search the house because we aren't cops with a search warrant. So just try to have faith that everything will work out. That's what I do. I believe that God will make it so we will be able to save Billy from whatever hell he's going through right now," Jim said, driving the car.

"I guess you're right... Poor kid, I can only imagine what he must have endured. And that's not even mentioning what it must be like for his parents... The only reason his parents hired us in the first place was because the police wouldn't do a thing but give them excuses."

"Yeah, I know it's terrible. But the least we can do is help find Billy when no one else will... Anyway, we're here," Jim said, parking on the right side of the roadway.

Exiting the car, the two looked around and could only see the forest surrounding them. It was nothing but woodlands for miles, which caused Connor to fidget with his trench coat. Seeing that it would be mostly forest around them, Jim double-checked the address. Meanwhile, Connor surveyed the area, searching through the twigs and bushes. Having no luck finding anything, he proceeded to look around the trees. Eventually, he did catch sight of a shoe beneath a tree log.

Following this, Connor and Jim set out in the direction of the shoe. After trudging through the damp forest, they came across an old wooden cabin. They also spotted a red pickup truck parked in front of the cabin, along with effigies made from sticks and human remains. Both of their eyes widened at the sight, leaving them both speechless.

"Well, I guess the address from the old man was correct after all," Connor remarked as they approached the cabin.

Using their flashlights, the two inspected the cabin's windows. Seeing that the cabin was vacant, Jim tried to open the cabin door, but found it to be locked. With the door locked, Connor stepped in and examined the door.

"This door seems worn down. Hmm, I'm going to try something, but I'd suggest you back up," Connor said, proceeding to kick the door down.

"Well, that's one way to open a door," Jim commented.

Now entering the cabin, they discovered a handcrafted shrine of what appeared to be a humanoid with a deer skull for a head. Candles surrounded the shrine, some of which were still lit. The shrine also looked like it was made from sticks and bones.

Continuing to investigate the interior of the cabin, they stumbled into another room with a pentagram drawn on the wooden floor in blood. The room also had hanging charms that seemed to be made from sticks. The two continued to search the cabin but found no sign of Billy.

"Damn it, where could this kid be? The only things we've managed to find are what I can assume to be a satanic shrine, some hanging sticks, and a pentagram. Which we should probably avoid touching," Connor said.

"I know. There must be *something* we're not seeing," Jim replied.

With Billy nowhere to be found, Connor thought of places where someone could hide a child. Wandering around the cabin looking for any clues, he noticed bloodstains on a green carpet. Removing the carpet, he'd discovered a cellar door.

Seeing the cellar door had a lock on it, Connor looked around for anything he could use. It wasn't long before he caught a glimpse of a hammer on top of a table nearby. Using the hammer, he struck the lock on the cellar door a few times until it broke.

Having the cellar door finally open, Connor called Jim, who came shortly. They found it pitch black, leading them to pull out their flashlights. Upon entering the cellar, they were met with a revolting smell.

"It smells like something died in here," Connor remarked.

"Connor, I'm afraid… that's an accurate deduction," Jim said, flashing his light to reveal mutilated animal and human corpses that were hung up on the wall.

Feeling nauseous from the sight, Connor said, "Whoever did this… is completely insane."

Scouring through the cellar, they heard mumbling nearby. The mumbling grew louder as they made their way through the cellar with their flashlights. Eventually, they found Billy with his arms tied to a pillar.

"Please… Just let me go home. I promise I won't tell anybody… Just let me go home," Billy said, with tears flowing down his face.

"Hey, don't be scared. We've come to rescue you," Connor said.

"What? Who… are you?"

"We're consulting detectives hired by your parents. They've been really worried about you, Billy," Jim explained while Connor freed Billy from his restraints.

As Jim helped Billy climb the cellar steps, Connor left the cellar first. However, he suddenly heard the floor creak behind him. Turning around, he'd be met with an axe swing that nearly missed him. Having seen the axe swinger, he could only assume it was Richard, wearing a black robe.

"No! You will not take him away from me!" Richard shouted, charging at Connor.

Connor evaded Richard's swings, which eventually led Richard to get his axe stuck in the wall. Richard tried to pull out his axe, but to no avail, as Connor swiftly knocked Richard out with a straight jab to the head. Having knocked out Richard, Connor, and Jim helped Billy exit the cabin safely.

"The police should be here any minute now. Do you want me to call your parents for you?" Jim asked.

"Umm... Yes, please, I would really like that... And thank you for finding me," Billy replied, wiping the tears off his face.

"I'm just glad we could help," Jim said, handing Billy his phone.

Meanwhile, Connor watched Richard, who he'd tied up with rope that he found nearby. Richard appeared to be still unconscious, which prompted him to reflect. *It's scary, knowing that just a single person's actions could easily ruin someone else's life. Only God would know what would've happened to Billy if we didn't get here in time.*

Coming back to his senses, he looked down and saw that Richard was gone. A chill ran down his spine as he began looking around for any sign of Richard. In the following seconds, he heard footsteps approaching him, which allowed him to dodge an axe hurled at him. Evading the axe once again, he would be tackled by Richard, who attempted to stab him with a knife.

"I must complete the mission that was given to me! I just need to perform one more sacrifice! So, I cannot allow you to take him away from me!" Richard shouted, struggling to stab Connor.

"What on earth are you talking about? You're insane!" Connor shouted back as he tossed Richard off him.

Once Connor had Richard pinned on the ground, he proceeded to punch Richard repeatedly, over and over again. This went on until Richard's face began to swell up and bleed. It was only until Jim stepped in and grabbed hold of his arm.

"Connor! You need to stop or else you will kill him!" Jim shouted.

Freezing up, Connor looked at Jim and, later, at Richard. Seeing Richard's battered face, he stepped back and looked at his bloodied hands. Jim placed his hand on Connor's shoulder and crouched down next to him.

"Hey, it's okay... You didn't mean to overdo it," Jim said.

"I almost killed him... I couldn't control myself. If it weren't for you... I would have just killed a man," Connor mumbled.

"I know, but what's important is that you stopped... Now, take this and get yourself cleaned up. We don't want the police finding you with blood on your hands," Jim said, handing Connor a blue handkerchief.

The police arrived shortly after and began collecting evidence from the cabin. Billy, meanwhile, was being checked by paramedics while talking with his parents on Jim's phone. Seeing this, Connor smiled, feeling like they had saved a life. As Connor stood there, Jim approached him and patted him on the shoulder.

"Hey umm, we need to talk," Jim said.

"Oh, what is it?" Connor replied.

"Well, I'm worried about you, son. What you did to that man moments ago is... frightening."

"I know. I'm sorry. It's just that sometimes I lash out and I can't control myself. But even if I did kill that... *monster*, he would've deserved it for everything he's done."

"No! Connor, you don't get to decide who gets to live and die. Only God does... even if they are monsters. I didn't teach you how to fight just so you can become a murderer. I taught you how to fight so you can *defend* yourself... Promise me that you will never think that way again."

"Okay, I promise... and I'm sorry," Connor said, as the two sat there in silence.

After a while, the two were about to leave, but Connor heard footsteps behind them. Turning to see who it was, they were greeted by another police officer. This officer, however, wore a slightly different uniform and carried a briefcase with him.

"Excuse me, but may I have a word with the two of you?" the Officer asked.

"Sorry, but we already explained everything to you officers. We have done our part in finding the kid—" Connor said but got interrupted.

"Actually, I am not here to talk about the case of Billy."

"Oh, then what are you here to talk about?"

"First, allow me to introduce myself. My name is James Willie. I am the current chief of police of Minneapolis, but you may call me Chief Willie if you want... And I need your help."

Chapter 2
A Killer on the Loose

At their investigation agency office, Jim prepared coffee for the three of them. Meanwhile, Connor and Chief Willie were sitting at a table. Pulling out a case file from his briefcase, Chief Willie presented it to Connor. Reviewing the case file, Connor's eyes widened, seeing the graphic photos taken of the mayor's wife's corpse.

"Yikes, you should've at least given me a warning… So, this all happened three days ago?" Connor asked.

"That's right, and as I've already said, I need your help," Chief Willie replied.

"Yeah, about that. That's what I'm having trouble understanding. Why come to us for help? We're just two consulting detectives trying to help the people of our hometown. So, I don't see why the *literal* chief of police of a city would need our help in finding your mayor."

"Well, we've been short on officers lately, and after seeing how quickly you found Billy, I'm sure we'll be able to find our mayor with your help in no time."

Contemplating Chief Willie's request, Connor tapped his finger on the table. Jim soon arrived with coffee and handed a cup to them both. With his coffee in hand, Jim sat down at the table and was about to take a sip.

Though, before Jim could sip his coffee, Connor interrupted him, "Hey, can we talk in private?"

"Huh? Oh, sure," Jim replied as the two made their way into another room.

Leaning against a wall, Connor shook his head and said, "I don't know Jim, I just have this *feeling* that we shouldn't do this case."

"What makes you say that?" Jim asked, taking a sip of coffee.

"Well, I can't describe it, but I get this bad feeling from him. I don't know, my point is, I think we should be focusing on helping the people of our town instead of a city that we don't have anything to do with."

"Hmm… There was this story your father told me when we both were in the *marines*. It was a Bible story called Parable of the Good Samaritan. The story was about a traveler who had been stripped of his clothing and left half dead on the ground by robbers. First, a Jewish priest passed by the traveler and ignored him, then a Levite came by, who also avoided the man. Finally, a humble Samaritan happened upon the traveler, and unlike those before him, he helped and cared for the traveler."

"I see, but why did the Samaritan help the traveler?"

"Well, this was a story originally told by Jesus Christ, he used the Samaritan as an example that people should care and help everyone, even your enemy. In other words, to love your neighbor, regardless of who they are."

After hearing this, Connor pondered his decision, gazing at Chief Willie through the office curtains. *I just know something about this chief isn't right. I just can't seem to figure out what that is. But maybe Jim's right...* Glancing around the office, he noticed a photo frame of his family. Seeing the photo, he wondered what they all would do in his place. Making his decision, Connor and Jim returned to Chief Willie, who finished his coffee.

"Okay, I've thought about it, and we'll help you find your mayor," Connor said.

"Yes, thank you. I can assure you that you won't regret this," Chief Willie replied.

"I hope not... So, where do we start?"

Now in Minneapolis, Connor, Jim, along with Chief Willie arrive at the mayor's apartment building. Coming into the building, Connor saw how luxurious the lobby was, with its floors made of marble. Once they reached the top floor via the elevator, they strolled through the hallways, approaching the mayor's penthouse.

Entering the penthouse, the first thing they saw was a blood-stained carpet floor. Following the blood, it led to the master bedroom, where they found a puddle of dried blood. Assuming that's where the mayor's wife was found dead, they continue to inspect the area.

Squatting down, Connor pulled out a magnifying glass and examined the floor. He noticed that it had multiple fingerprints. He also noticed a trail of blood that led to the living room. He assumed that the mayor held his wife's body before going to the living room.

"If it helps, I'll tell you both everything we've found so far. When we began investigating, we learned that before Mayor Johnson left city hall, he was approached by a journalist named Briana Harper. She asked the mayor a question about a conspiracy that may or may not be true," Chief Willie explained, while Connor and Jim inspected the crime scene.

"Interesting, what was the conspiracy about?" Connor asked.

"Well, after questioning some eyewitnesses, the conspiracy the journalist mentioned was a series of murders of government officials that was supposedly all done by this serial killer that's been dubbed as *The Mortem*... But it's all just rumors."

"Hmm, okay, so this Mortem has a pattern. They specifically target government officials... So why did they change their pattern now? Instead of killing the mayor, they kidnapped him. But they also killed his wife who isn't any kind of city official... Perhaps we should think about what is motivating this Mortem in the first place. Is their motive political? Or maybe it's... personal," Jim speculated.

"If only we had a witness, it might make solving this much easier," Connor said, gazing upon the city through the penthouse's window view.

"Oh, actually there is a witness we may be able to talk to... Let me just make a call," Chief Willie said, dialing a number on his phone.

Finishing up at the mayor's penthouse, the three now head over to an orphanage in the suburbs of Minneapolis. Arriving at the orphanage, they saw children running around and playing tag in its playground. With a puzzled look on their faces, Connor and Jim were welcomed by an elderly woman.

"Hello, my name is Hannah, the administrator of this orphanage. What can I help you with?"

"Yes, hello Hannah. We spoke on the phone earlier today, remember? We're here to see Amelia," Chief Willie said.

"Oh yes, I remember! My apologies. It's just that we have so many children being orphaned this year that it has been very difficult for me to keep track of everything. Anyway, follow me and I'll show you to Amelia's room... Poor girl, she has just lost both her parents, so please be patient with her," Hannah said, leading them.

Arriving at Amelia's room, they entered and saw Amelia huddled on her bed. Gazing out the window, Amelia also held onto a teddy bear she had clutched in her arms. Approaching Amelia, Chief Willie crouched in front of her, greeting her.

"Hello Amelia, how are you adjusting to life here?" Chief Willie asked.

"It's... okay, I guess," Amelia said, looking down at her teddy bear.

"I see, well anyway, these two are Connor and Jim. They are helping me to find your father and to find out who... took your mother away. We came here to ask you some questions if that's alright with you?"

Seeing Amelia nod to Chief Willie, Connor sat down beside her and said, "Hi Amelia. As you already know, my name is Connor. Now, can you please tell me what happened or at least what you can remember about... that night?"

"Well, I remember waking up after hearing a lot of shooting... When I left my room to see what was happening, I found my mom dead in my parents' room... I didn't know what to do or what was happening but then I heard my dad yelling in the living room. When I went to see what was happening there, I saw him trying to fight a hooded man that broke into our penthouse. The hooded man was hitting my dad with a baseball bat, and after that, he injected him with something… After that, my dad fell asleep and then the hooded man took out a garbage bag which he put my dad inside of and finally left."

"Oh my God… Okay umm, thank you, Amelia. I'm so sorry that we're making you have to remember such an *awful* event. But because you're telling us this, it's helping us be able to bring whoever did this to justice," Connor said as they all left Amelia's room.

Now leaving the orphanage, Connor contemplated Amelia's story. *Was what she said reliable? Children often tell the truth, so there's a chance it may be. But why did The Mortem leave Amelia alive? Could he have a soft spot for children?* With so many questions running through his mind, he then thought of something that may give them some insight.

"Hey chief, you mentioned that before the mayor left city hall, he was approached by that journalist Briana, right? Well, how about we give Briana a visit and ask her some questions about this so-called Mortem?"

Having finished at the orphanage, the three traversed to an old apartment building west of Minneapolis downtown. On their way there, they drove through a neighborhood that looked ruined. However, Connor's eyes widened when he saw multiple posters hung up for cosmetics. Though what caught his attention was that they featured the mayor's wife on them.

"Hey chief, what's with the posters that are hung up everywhere?" Connor asked.

"Ah, that's Martha's cosmetics company. I remember that she once showed me how she tested her cosmetics for them to be safe for the public… She apparently hired the homeless to test her cosmetics."

"Wait, isn't that a bit inhumane? What if those untested cosmetics permanently injure those poor people?"

"Kinda, but I believe otherwise since most of those homeless would have starved if Martha hadn't hired them. In fact, some actually enjoyed working for her since it was the only way they could earn enough to live on."

"I guess. It still feels wrong though, knowing they were being used for such a selfish purpose… Anyway, we've arrived."

Going up the stairs of the building, Connor noticed the wall's cracked paint, followed by some graffiti. Connor also heard people arguing echo throughout the building. Reaching the floor where the journalist lived, they stood in a long hallway.

Reaching the reporter's apartment, Connor knocked three times on her door. With no answer, he looked down at the doorknob and saw it damaged. Pushing the door, he discovered that the door was open. Glancing into the apartment, he checked to see if there was anyone inside.

"Hello? Is anyone home? Briana Harper, can we come in? We just want to ask you a few questions—" Connor said but caught a glimpse of a corpse lying dead on the floor.

Afterward, officers inspected the apartment, collecting evidence. Meanwhile, Connor and Jim examined Briana's corpse and saw that she had her throat sliced open. They also noticed that her arm had a cut on it where she appeared to have bled out a lot.

Despite Briana's horrific murder, Connor couldn't help scratching his head over the fact that her corpse was inside a pentagram. The pentagram seemed to have been drawn with the blood from Briana's cut on her arm. There were also unlit candles surrounding the perimeter of the pentagram that gave off the smell of vanilla.

The sight made Connor take two small steps backward, witnessing what he can assume to have been a sacrifice. Examining the scene, he was reminded of what they had seen in the cabin where they found Billy. *Could there be a connection between the two? Perhaps it was done by the same kind of insane people?* Although he was unsure what to make out what had happened, he knew there was something strange happening.

"What an awful way to die," Jim remarked.

"You can say that again... Hey, what's that on her forehead? It kind of looks like The Star of David with... an eye in the center?" Connor said, lifting Briana's bangs.

"This was no murder... It was a sacrifice," Jim muttered, gazing upon the unlit candles surrounding them.

As the two inspected Briana's corpse, they were soon approached by Chief Willie. Chief Willie squatted down and gazed upon Briana's corpse. Frowning at the sight, Chief Willie sighed.

"Just how many more innocent people will The Mortem kill?" Chief Willie said, standing back up.

"Wait, you think The Mortem did this?" Jim asked.

"Well, of course, I do. Who else could it have been? She was investigating The Mortem's murders. Don't you think that's enough reason for The Mortem to kill her?"

"I mean, yeah, that does sorta make sense... But she's not a government official, so why would The Mortem now start killing civilians? Plus, her murder looks like it was a sacrifice, which does not line up with how The Mortem killed the mayor's wife," Connor clarified.

"Even so, it doesn't change the fact that this woman was murdered... I wonder if she has something that could still give us some insight about what happened?" Chief Willie said, glancing around the apartment.

Walking away from the corpse of Briana, Connor proceeded to inspect the apartment. Roaming around the apartment, he noticed a shoe print on the seat of a chair. The chair was in front of a bookshelf that had a couple of novels and dictionaries. *Someone must have been frequently stepping onto this chair, to have left that print. I wonder what's up on that bookshelf.* Stepping on top of the chair, he found a journal on the roof of the bookshelf.

Reading through the journal, Connor discovered notes about the series of murders committed by The Mortem. Some of the notes discussed what happened in each murder and how they connected. Other notes talked about another conspiracy about human trafficking.

"Hey chief, you might want to take a look at this," Connor said, showing Chief Willie the journal.

"Human trafficking? Could this be connected to The Mortem killings?" Chief Willie inquired.

"Maybe, it looks like she was searching for possible connections. For instance, take a look at this," Connor said, pointing out notes and photos of a casino.

"That's The Royal Chalice, it's a casino downtown central. It's also owned by one of the biggest kingpins of the city… Mr. Dixon," Chief Willie explained.

"Hmm, you think he'd be the type to meddle in human trafficking?" Connor asked.

"It's likely because Mr. Dixon does have a history in the black market. Another thing about Mr. Dixon is that he considers himself a businessman and is not the kindest of souls."

Now back at the police station, Connor jotted down on a whiteboard, trying to piece together clues. Meanwhile, Jim skimmed through Briana's journal. Doing so, he came across a goodbye message that appeared to have been written in a hurry.

If someone finds this journal, I beg you to bring awareness to the issues that my notes in this journal raise and to use the evidence I've gathered. They've found me. I don't know how they found me, but I will probably not be alive by the time anyone finds this. I'm so sorry mom, dad I love you both… Goodbye world.

After reading Briana's heartbreaking goodbye message, Jim took a moment of silence to process what he read. Following that, he walked around the police station office and saw Connor jotting on the whiteboard. Sitting down on a chair nearby, he turned to look at Connor.

"Can I ask you something?" Jim asked.

"Sure, what is it?" Connor replied, still jotting on the whiteboard.

"Well, I've just been wondering… Why are you still doing this? This detective work has become an obsession lately. If I recall correctly, you didn't even want to do this job originally."

"We've been over this Jim. You know why I'm still doing it…"

"I know, and I know I'm not your father, but if he was here, he'd want you to move on and become someone. I'm just worried about you Connor. I also know your mother and Michael would want that for you as well. Please, Connor, it's been three years since they all…"

"Okay, so you're saying I should just quit and go to law school, maybe become a lawyer? Find a woman who loves me and start a family? Ever since I lost them, my life has been meaningless! I couldn't live with myself if I were to just move on! It's not that easy, Jim… What I'm doing is keeping their memory alive!"

Following that, the room fell into a deep silence. There were no further words spoken, and only the ticking of the clock could be heard. The two stayed in silence for some time until Chief Willie entered the room.

"We just received a call from a motel located downtown east… They claim to have found Mayor Johnson," Chief Willie explained.

Now making their way to the motel, Connor gazed out the police car window. Observing the people in the neighborhood, he'd see people rummaging through garbage cans and dumpsters. He also saw children and elderly using rusty metal sheets to stay dry from the rain in makeshift campsites.

While they drove through the area, suddenly, trash was thrown against the car's window. People were shouting as they continued throwing trash at the police car. Chief Willie, however, wasn't fazed and just continued driving.

"Hey, shouldn't we do something?" Connor asked.

"Don't bother, this is how it usually is in this part of the city."

"Really? Well, if you say so. Anyway, could you tell us how the mayor was found? You kinda left that part vague."

"Well, according to what the woman said on the phone, she's a housekeeper at this motel. She found the mayor in one of the rooms, and based on the tone of her voice, the odds of the mayor being alive ain't looking good."

Upon arriving, the motel was overrun with police cars and ambulances. While the three stepped out of the police car, Connor caught a glance of the housekeeper. Sobbing, the housekeeper had police officers trying to calm her down. When approaching the room door, Chief Willie spoke to one of the officers.

"Okay, give it to me briefly," Chief Willie said.

"Forgive me chief but none of us have gone inside yet, except for Johnny," the Officer clarified.

"I see, so where is Johnny then?" Chief Willie asked.

"I'm not sure, I haven't seen him in a while. He might still be inside."

"Hmm, alright, let's have a look now, shall we?"

When the three entered the room, the stench of death engulfed the air. Walking into the room, Connor felt nauseated, seeing the blood-stained carpet. He glanced around the room, where he found a trail of blood leading into the bathroom.

Connor gulped when walking toward the bathroom, but as he did, he heard some noise coming from the closet. Connor, however, shrugged this off and continued walking. The more he got closer to the bathroom, the stench grew stronger.

Opening the bathroom room, he shined his flashlight into the dimly lit bathroom. There he found a bucket filled with human fingers. Next to it was a half-empty bottle of bleach. Continuing to look inside, he discovered Mayor Johnson half-naked, seated on a chair facing the bathroom mirror. He later placed his hand close to the mayor's mouth, checking to see if the mayor was breathing.

Feeling that the mayor wasn't exhaling, Connor now knew that the mayor was gone. Inspecting the mayor, he found that the mayor's wrists were tied to the chair's armrest. He also noticed that the mayor had all his fingers missing along with numerous burns and bruises on his back.

Stepping away from the mayor's corpse, Connor was called by Jim. Exiting the bathroom, he found Jim, analyzing a bulletin board. On the bulletin board, he noticed several newspapers that discussed the controversy over Mayor Johnson's decision to raise the city's taxes. Next to the newspapers, he also saw various photos that consisted of people who appeared to look important. Further analyzing the photos, to his surprise, both Mayor Johnson's and Chief Willie's photos were present. Trying to interpret the bulletin board, they were later approached by Chief Willie.

"So, what did you two find?" Chief Willie asked.

"Well, we found the mayor, but he's…"

"I see… Johnson was a good friend of mine; I just can't believe this is how he goes."

"Yeah, I know the feeling… Anyway, regarding this bulletin board, I'm not sure what to think, but based on these photos, I'm guessing these people are The Mortem's next targets," Connor explained.

"That's right, but these photos not only include Mayor Johnson… but they also include you," Jim further clarified.

"Heh, would you look at that, it does. Oh, now that's interesting, his other targets are all members of the city council."

Afterward, the three stood outside, discussing their next move. Meanwhile, Connor contemplated everything he had seen in the motel room. However, in the corner of his eye, he caught a glimpse of a police officer exiting the motel room they were just at. Squinting his eyes, he received a chill down his spine, realizing who that could be.

"Hey, excuse me! Yeah, I'm talking to you… May I ask what you're doing there, pal?" Connor shouted at the officer, but the officer kept quiet.

"… Johnny is that you?" Chief Willie asked, but also got no response.

As the officer stood there motionless, Chief Willie slowly reached for his pistol. However, the officer turned around and fired three bullets, shooting two officers. Panic then ensued with the officer who shot the three bullets fleeing into an alleyway nearby.

Witnessing the two officers being killed right before his eyes, Connor clenched his fists and jaw. The pursuit commenced as he chased the officer into the alley. Chasing the officer, he saw many homeless people sheltering in the alleyways. Having searched the alley for some time, he became soaked by the rain that poured down on him. Continuing to search the alley, he eventually came across a knocked-out man.

Connor noticed a bruise on the man's head and saw a police coat thrown on the ground nearby. *Looks like I'm getting close… Now where could this guy have gone?* Looking around, he spotted an opened door that led into a building nearby.

Entering the building, Connor prowled through the hallways. Doing so, he witnessed a man wearing a raincoat heading up the stairwell. Pursuing the man, he tried to glance up ahead, but received two gunshots from the man in the raincoat.

Fortunately, Connor managed to evade the many gunshots raining down on him, with many nearly hitting him. At that moment, the man in the raincoat aimed one last time at Connor. However, when the man pulled the trigger, no shot was fired. Seeing this, Connor chuckled, watching the man fleeing to the roof.

Arriving on the roof, an exhausted Connor inspected the area, but his eyebrows lifted when he discovered himself to be the only one there. Fatigue now obscuring his vision, he heard footsteps approaching behind him. When Connor turned around, he got a hefty blow to the side of his head.

As a result, Connor plummeted to the floor, where he had his ribs kicked. Having his hair grabbed, the man in the raincoat proceeded to smash his face two times on the floor. In a fit of rage, Connor responded by elbowing the man. This caused the man to let go, allowing him to then pin the man down.

"Okay pal, the chase is over!" Connor shouted, holding up a fist.

No words were spoken by the man as the man hid his face with the raincoat's hood. Attempting to see what the man looked like, Connor was suddenly head-butted by the man, becoming unconscious. Standing back up, the man spat out blood on the floor and began to reload his pistol.

With a pistol fully loaded, the man pressed it to the side of Connor's head. As the man was about to pull the trigger, Connor unconsciously turned his face towards the man. Upon seeing Connor's face, the man suddenly paused. Looking at his pistol, the man began to tremble all over, causing him to lose grip on his pistol. After that, the man clenched his head with both his hands and fell to his knees.

Connor eventually regained consciousness and when he did, he looked around to see the man in the raincoat nowhere to be found. Inspecting the area, he found himself alone. However, he did stumble upon the pistol that the man had dropped on the floor. Contemplating why the man didn't kill him, he raised one eyebrow, wondering why he was still alive. Now exiting the building, he heard Chief Willie calling out his name, who shortly arrived.

"Connor, what happened? Did you see his face?" Chief Willie asked.

"No, I wasn't able to... and I think he got away," Connor replied.

"Hmm, are you sure? You didn't get a small glimpse of it?"   "I'm sorry but no. The whole time he was covering it with a hood and was looking away.

"I see... Anyway, let's head back, there might still be some evidence in that motel room we can use to find him. Don't worry, we'll get him next time."

"Yeah... next time."

Chapter 3
Sterling's Party

Returning to the motel, Connor saw paramedics attempting to revive the two officers who got shot. He couldn't stand the sight, resulting in him looking away. Shifting his gaze, he saw the motel room and noticed paramedics carrying an injured officer to an ambulance.

"What happened to him?" Connor inquired.

"Not sure, let's go find out," Chief Willie said as they both approached the paramedics.

Walking up to the paramedics Chief Willie asked, "Excuse me but do you mind telling us what happened to my fellow officer?"

"Ah, well we found the officer inside the closet of the motel room. He was unconscious and by the looks of his head injury, I say he has a severe concussion," explained one of the paramedics.

After hearing this, Connor came to realize it was The Mortem who made the noise in the closet. Seeing that the injured officer had his police coat missing, it explained why The Mortem had one. To show respect, Connor crossed himself, shedding some tears. However, while he stood there, he heard Jim shouting out his name. As soon as he turned around, Jim suddenly grabbed hold of him.

"Don't you ever do something like that again! Who do you think you are? You can't just chase after a serial killer!" Jim shouted, tearing up.

"I'm sorry—" Connor said but got cut off from Jim.

"I don't care if you're sorry! You could have died for God's sake!"

"I know… Forgive me Jim but right now I can't do this… I need some air," Connor said, walking away.

Following Connor's departure, Jim turned to Chief Willie and asked, "So, what's next for this case?"

"Well, now that we've found the mayor, I think we can take over from here… But, if you both want to continue helping, all the better." Chief Willie clarified.

"I see… I'll have to ask Connor what he thinks we should do… I do feel bad about yelling at him… This is the first time he's actually *seen* someone get murdered."

A few days later, Connor was standing out on a balcony. He gazed over the city and watched the people on the streets. *It really is scary how fragile life can be… You can be living your life thinking nothing bad will ever happen, but that all could change in an instant.* Wiping the tears from his eyes, he went back inside and saw Jim tying his tie.

"Are you alright? You look like you just saw a ghost," Jim said, noticing Connor's expression.

"Oh, yeah, I'm fine. I was just daydreaming... Anyway, I still can't believe that Chief Willie managed to get us this five-star hotel room."

"I know, but now that the mayor has been found, there's no need for us to keep working on this case. Plus, we weren't even the ones who found the mayor, a housekeeper did."

"Yeah, but after seeing what The Mortem did to all those people. I can't help but think of how badly I want him to get brought to justice... So that's why I want to keep working on the case until that happens.

"Okay, but please Connor, don't do anything stupid like how you chased after The Mortem into the alleyways... You're lucky you didn't get killed. Anyway, get dressed. We have a funeral to attend."

Arriving at the city cemetery, Connor and Jim saw a large crowd trying to enter, but security guards blocked the way. Once they exited their car, they were both noticed by the crowd of people. Realizing these people were the press, they became surrounded by them.

"Excuse me sir, but what are your thoughts on whether the mayor's decision is still valid after his death?" one of the reporters asked but before either one of them could get a word out, Chief Willie stepped in and escorted the two to the mayor's burial.

"I'm so sorry for that, but ever since word got out that Mayor Johnson is dead, the press has been at it nonstop," Chief Willie explained.

"It's fine, I can imagine it must be very exhausting," said Connor.

"Oh, trust me you have no idea. But anyway, there's someone I want you both to meet," Chief Willie said, presenting them to a man in a black suit with a white tie.

Glancing at the man, Connor noticed his strangely pale skin. Shaking the man's hand, he felt how cold the man was to the touch. As a result, Connor's eyes widened, feeling like he was touching something frozen.

"Hey, are you alright?" Connor asked.

"Oh, my apology. I was born with a rare hereditary condition that makes my body temperature colder than the average person... The name is Charles Sterling by the way. Though, my friends call me Sterling."

"Ah, well I'm Connor, this is Jim. We're both consulting detectives... Also, you look a bit familiar."

"That's because Sterling here was among the many photos that were pinned on the bulletin board at The Mortem's motel room. Seeing as he is a member of the Minneapolis City Council, I felt that he deserved to know what was going on in the case," Chief Willie explained.

"Indeed, but I am currently the only member who knows, and I'd like to keep it that way for now. I don't want the other council members to worry about this… Mortem."

"I see, and I'm guessing the press is also in the dark about The Mortem?" Jim asked.

"That's right, some rumors are floating around, but nothing we should be worried about," Chief Willie replied.

After that, Connor was caught by a strong breeze that blew against him. This led to him noticing Amelia arriving at the funeral and being accompanied by Hannah. Seeing Amelia visiting her parents' coffins made him remember the time he also grieved at his family's funeral. Approaching Amelia, he crouched next to her and greeted her.

"Hello again, how are you holding up?" Connor asked Amelia, who was clutching onto a white rose.

"… What do you think?" Amelia said, wiping away tears from her eyes.

"Listen, I know what it's like to lose your family… And to know the feeling of being alone in the world. But the truth is, as long as you have people that care about you. People that you can consider family, then you're never really alone," Connor said, glancing at Jim.

Sniffling between her words, Amelia said, "You think I'll be able to find people… like that?"

"I know you can… but it all depends on you if you're willing to accept those people into your life."

Hearing what Connor explained to her, Amelia smiled and proceeded to hug Connor. Leaving the white rose on her parents' coffin, Amelia was escorted away by Hannah as they left the funeral. Seeing the mayor and his wife's coffins, Connor crossed himself, showing respect to the deceased. However, he gasped when Sterling patted him on his back.

"Are you Christian?" Sterling asked.

"Huh? Oh, no I'm Catholic, actually. But then again, all Catholics are Christian but not all Christians are Catholic. Speaking of which, are you religious, by any chance?"

"I am… in a sense."

"I see. I know it's hard to believe sometimes, but my mom used to say that God's timing is perfect. Meaning when something happens, including when something *bad* happens, it's all for a reason…"

A moment of silence soon took place, with only birds chirping being heard. Gazing over the mayor's burial, Connor reminisced about the day when he and Jim were at his family's funeral. Eventually, he came back to his senses, hearing Sterling call out his name.

"Connor, you okay there? You're… crying," Sterling said.

"Huh? I am?" Connor said, touching his face, feeling tears flowing down his cheeks.

"I can tell that you're emotional when it comes to funerals."

"Heh, guess I am. Don't know what came over me," said Connor, wiping his tears away.

"I see, anyhow when James explained to me the details of the case, he said that you all have been having trouble catching this Mortem. So, I have a proposition… What if I help bring this killer to justice?"

Afterward, at the station, Sterling jotted down on a whiteboard. Meanwhile, both Connor and Jim were seated on chairs with puzzled looks on their faces. When Sterling finished jotting down on the whiteboard, he turned to face the three.

"Okay, if we want to catch The Mortem, we need to understand his motives. Now, what are his motives? Well, we may not know all of them, but we do know one, and it's that he's out for blood for any who has some sort of position of power or is a politician. So, I propose that we bait him."

"Bait him? Are you suggesting that we use you as bait?" Jim asked.

"No, not *just* me. What I'm suggesting is that we use every person in power that lives in Minneapolis as bait. The plan is simple, I will host a party at my manor in honor of Mayor Johnson. I will send an invite to every powerful person I know in the city."

"Okay, and how will we know if The Mortem will show up?" Chief Willie asked.

"Well, it's not guaranteed that he'll show up, but I'll give the three of you a list of the people I'll invite, along with their photos. Also, as a way for us to communicate with each other, we'll be using *these* earpieces. Now, if someone shows up and is not on the list, we just might have our culprit."

In the days that followed, the three went along with Sterling's plan. And on the day of the party Connor, Jim, and Chief Willie watched those who arrived at Sterling's manor from above a balcony. Meanwhile, Sterling was below, welcoming those who arrived. While doing this, Sterling was greeted by a woman that wore a golden necklace along with a violet silk dress.

"Sterling, how have you been?"

"My dear Nancy, you look gorgeous, and as for me, I've been doing fine, thank you very much," Sterling said, escorting Nancy inside.

"Oh Sterling, I'm flattered, but you know, when you announced that you were going to be hosting a party in honor of Johnson, I was honestly shocked. Considering you *despised* him the most out of the council. So may I ask, what are you up to?" Nancy inquired.

"Don't you worry, you'll find out soon enough. But anyway, how is work? I can imagine being Minneapolis's District Attorney must be a struggle for you, considering that there's so much crime nowadays."

"Ah, so it's going to be like that? Well, as for being this city's district attorney, it has been challenging with the abundance of crime. Though, I've been getting used to it."

"I see, well this was a nice chat and all but I'm afraid I must go. I have other matters to attend to," Sterling said, bidding Nancy farewell with a kiss on the hand.

Meanwhile, Connor, Jim, and Chief Willie were now below, inspecting those from afar. They'd take glances at the guests' faces, confirming whether they were on the list or not. Doing so, the three conversed with each other with the earpieces Sterling gave to them.

"Hey, are you guys having any luck? Because so far everyone appears to have been invited," Connor said, lying against a wall.

"Unfortunately, it's the same for me. I don't know, but using these people as bait doesn't sit right with me," Jim replied.

"I know none of this feels morally right, but it's necessary if we want to catch The Mortem," Chief Willie clarified.

"But is it necessary? There's got to be a better way than what we're doing," Jim replied.

Upon hearing what Chief Willie and Jim said, Connor began to ponder. *What are we doing? Does Jim have a point about what we're doing being okay? I don't want to put any of these people in danger just so we could catch some serial killer.* Fidgeting with his tie, Connor began taking deep breaths as he continued checking the guest. However, he gasped when he felt a pat on his shoulder. Turning to see who it was, it turned out to be Sterling, who held onto a glass of wine.

"Forgive me, did I startle you?" Sterling said.

"Oh, nah I'm just a bit nervous that's all. It's not every day you're spending the night at a high-class party," Connor replied.

"Heh, I see. So, did you find someone who is not on the list yet?" Sterling asked.

"Not yet, so far everyone appears to have been invited. I don't know Sterling; it doesn't look like he'll show up."

"He'll show up. I know he will, it's just a matter of time. Anyhow, do you want a tour of my manor?"

"Oh, umm sure I'd like that."

Now giving a tour to Connor, Sterling led Connor to a hallway of paintings. The paintings were hung up on walls and varied from a city to a cabin in the woods. Connor stopped to gaze at the paintings, but the painting of the cabin in the wood caught his attention.

"I see you're fond of fiară cabină. You know, I painted this one myself. In fact, every painting here was painted by a member of my family," Sterling said.

"Really? Well, I see you come from a family of artists," Connor remarked.

"Yes, that we are… You know, James told me that you had an encounter with The Mortem. Did you happen to see his face? Did it seem *familiar* to you?"

"Umm, no? I wouldn't know because I never got to see his face… I already told Chief Willie that. Didn't he tell you?"

"Hmm, I'm afraid he didn't mention that part… My apologies."

"… Anyway, umm, I'm sorry, but I can't take it anymore. Using these people as bait… It just feels wrong to be doing this kind of thing—" Connor said but got cut off when they suddenly heard gunfire.

On their way to investigate where the gunfire came from, they found the guests frightened. Glancing up ahead, Connor saw a bulky man wearing a gray suit with a brown tie. The bulky man had a group of men as bodyguards. The bodyguards were also all carrying automatic rifles.

"Who is that?" Connor asked.

"That's Mr. Dixon… He wasn't supposed to be here. I'm going to go see what he wants, you stay here," Sterling said, walking up to Mr. Dixon.

As Sterling approached Mr. Dixon, he greeted him with a handshake. The two shook hands while trading glares at each other. After that, they sat down at a table nearby.

"So, what brings you here Frederick? I don't recall inviting you… or your men," said Sterling.

"What's with the attitude Charles? I thought we were on good terms. Considering what you *people* did to me… Anyway, as soon as I heard that you were going to host a party in honor of our late mayor, I just had to come and see it for myself."

"Well, you saw it. Now please leave, your guns are scaring my guests."

"Have some patience Charles, I didn't come here solely to disturb the peace. In fact, I came here to renew our prior deal from before," Mr. Dixon said as he pulled out a red folder and handed it to Sterling.

When Sterling read the folder, his eyes widened. Noticing Sterling's expression, Mr. Dixon chuckled. Speechless, Sterling tapped his finger on the table.

"What do you want?" Sterling asked.

"Like I said, I want to renew the deal, but if you're not willing to cooperate... I'll *personally* expose you, people," replied Mr. Dixon.

"You wouldn't. You're not the kind to take a risk like that."

"Are you sure about that? You already know what I have on you people, given our history. With the snap of my fingers, I can expose you all to the world. Now, are you willing to cooperate or not?"

"... Keep dreaming Frederick," Sterling said, glaring.

"I'm disappointed Charles... I didn't want it to come to this, but you've given me no choice," Mr. Dixon said as he stood up and pulled out a pistol.

Shooting Sterling in the shoulder, this resulted in everyone in the manor panicking. With chaos ensuing, Mr. Dixon's guards blocked all the manor's exits. Following this, Chief Willie confronted Mr. Dixon, aiming his pistol at Mr. Dixon.

"Put the gun down! You put it down right now!" Chief Willie shouted but became surrounded by Mr. Dixon's guards.

"You better watch out James, or else my men here will put a bullet in you if you don't get out of my way... Hmm, on second thought, maybe I should just make an example of you—," said Mr. Dixon, taking aim at Chief Willie, but was punched in the face.

Plummeting to the floor, Mr. Dixon looked up and saw Connor standing before him. Connor stood there, staring down at Mr. Dixon. While he stood there, Mr. Dixon's bodyguards surrounded Connor and aimed at him, awaiting their next orders.

"You punched me... Do you have any idea what you've just done? Do you have any idea who I am!" Mr. Dixon shouted, standing back up.

"I know who you are. You're the guy who thinks that just because you have a lot of money and power means you can do *whatever* you want. But guess what, no one is above the law... and you just committed attempted murder."

"Haha, is that so? Don't shoot this one... because he's mine," Mr. Dixon said, grabbing Connor by the head and smashing it onto a table.

Due to the impact, Connor felt lightheaded as he tried walking, eventually collapsing to the floor. Mr. Dixon then got on top of him and grasped onto his neck, choking him. The weight of Mr. Dixon caused him to struggle to breathe under the pressure. It felt as though he couldn't move as he longed to breathe.

"Jim! Help me please!" Connor shouted but would be futile as Jim was nowhere in sight.

Connor tried kicking and punching Mr. Dixon, but it was all in vain. It seemed as though everything he could do was pointless; all he could do was struggle to get free. Just as Connor was about to lose consciousness, Mr. Dixon heard Sterling call out to him.

"Please… don't kill him! I'll agree to renew the deal, just don't kill him," Sterling said, bleeding.

Seeing Sterling beg, Mr. Dixon chuckled as he held Connor by his neck. Tossing Connor to the side, Mr. Dixon walked and approached Sterling. Looking at Sterling in the eye, Mr. Dixon took out a cigar and lit it with a lighter.

"Now, was that so hard? Considering that you're bleeding out, I'll come by the hospital in a week to renew the deal… Alright, we'll be leaving now, so you don't need to worry about us disturbing the peace any longer," Mr. Dixon said, smoking his cigar as he and his bodyguards left the manor.

Afterward, ambulances arrived at the manor, and paramedics rushed inside to take Sterling to an ambulance. Meanwhile, Connor sat on one of the ambulances and had an ice bag that he applied to his head. Soon after, Jim came over and sat down next to him.

"… Where were you?" Connor asked.

"Connor, I'm so sorry, but I had… a situation," Jim replied.

"Situation? Jim, I almost died, and Sterling almost died. What on earth could've been more important than me getting choked to death?" Connor shouted but noticed a horrified expression from Jim.

"Again, I'm sorry… Please understand that I would never abandon—" Jim said but got cut off by Connor.

"No, it's okay. I'm sorry I shouldn't have snapped at you like that… Anyway, let's go check on how Sterling is doing."

On their way to see Sterling, they saw Sterling whispering something to Chief Willie. Although Connor found it strange, he dismissed it. Once they arrived, Chief Willie greeted them.

"I'm so glad to see both of you alive! Connor, how is your head? If it weren't for you, I could've died," said Chief Willie.

"It's better now, but it still hurts. Anyhow, Sterling, are you okay?"

"I still have that bullet inside me, but the paramedics say that I'll be fine."

"Thank God it was your shoulder that was shot and not anywhere else… Though, I do have a question. What exactly was that deal you had with Mr. Dixon?"

"… Let's just say it was a deal involving some business I and old Dixon used to have. I ended that deal due to him wanting more money, which caused a bit of *conflict* between me and him."

"I see, and you mentioned that you didn't invite him. So, does that mean he's The Mortem? Or at least maybe he's the one paying him to murder these government officials?"

Contemplating the theory, Connor recalled what they had found in Briana's journal and began to connect some dots. Doing so, he noticed Jim being strangely silent on the subject. However, he shrugged it off once the paramedics arrived. When the paramedics were ready to take Sterling to the hospital, the four said their goodbyes.

After all the guests, along with Chief Willie, had left, Connor and Jim remained outside Sterling's manor. Gazing upon the city, Connor reflected on everything that had taken place since they arrived in Minneapolis. Now that Sterling was injured, he knew it was up to the three of them to crack the case. However, after facing Mr. Dixon, it helped convince him that the claims of Briana Harper against Mr. Dixon could very well be true.

Nonetheless, Connor began to wonder if there was more to Briana's journal than met the eye. *Why was Briana killed? Was it really The Mortem? There have been five murders already and we still don't know who the real killer is.* Every time he had a question answered, he had even more questions than before. Coming back to his senses, he glanced at Jim, who was smoking a cigarette.

"Hey, didn't you quit smoking?" Connor asked.

"Oh, uh, I did but I'm just a little stressed after everything that's happened," Jim replied.

"Heh, yeah, I know what you mean. Wow, what a view! No wonder Sterling had his manor on top of this hill, overseeing the city… By the way, what was that situation of yours? You know, when you disappeared?"

"Oh, um, it was… nothing. But I am sorry Connor, I should've been there."

"Hmm, nah, it's alright. It was me who almost got myself killed… But even so, we still need to find out who The Mortem is. He has already killed the mayor along with his wife, the journalist Briana, and two police officers. We need to catch this guy before he kills anyone else, but after tonight, Mr. Dixon seems to be hiding something. I bet that he's the one employing The Mortem to be his hitman."

"… Mr. Dixon may very well be the one hiring The Mortem, and there's also the fact that he could be conducting human trafficking at his casino… but we need proof," said Jim, tossing his used cigarette to the ground.

"Well, if we're gonna take down Mr. Dixon, we have to work together… So, no disappearing on me, okay?"

"Yes, and that's a promise... we're partners after all."

Chapter 4
The People vs. Frederick Dixon

The next day, Connor and Jim headed to the city's courthouse. When they arrived at the courthouse, they saw Chief Willie waiting for them outside. After exiting their car, they were greeted by Chief Willie.

"Good afternoon, I'm glad you both were able to come at such short notice," Chief Willie said, leading the way inside the courthouse.

"Yeah, of course, chief, but umm… why are we meeting here exactly?" Connor asked.

"Well, after last night's incident, I've been thinking of ways we can ruin Mr. Dixon. You also told me that little theory of yours that Mr. Dixon could be hiring The Mortem. So, I've come up with a plan." Chief Willie explained.

"I see, and what are you planning?" Jim asked.

"Before I answer that, I want you both to meet someone first… She's a good friend of mine," Chief Willie said, opening the doors of the courtroom.

On entering the courtroom, Connor saw what appeared to be an elderly woman facing off against a man wearing a high-end suit. As the trial unfolded, he wondered what events had caused the lawsuit. Turning to glance at Chief Willie, he thought that perhaps he would know.

"Hey chief, could you explain what's happening?" Connor asked.

"Well, I may not know all the details of the trial, but to sum it up Mrs. Lopez had filed a lawsuit against Arnold Scott, who's the owner of a paper company. So basically, Arnold wanted to buy Mrs. Lopez's house so he could have it bulldozed, but she kept on refusing his offer," Chief Willie explained.

Having learned this, Connor quietly rooted for Mrs. Lopez's victory. Soon after, the judge of the room began to bang her gavel, sending the courtroom into silence. As the judge prepared to speak, she cleared her throat and placed her microphone near her mouth.

"Okay, I have made my decision. Mrs. Lopez, you have indeed proven to me that Arnold has been wrongfully pressuring you into selling your house when you have refused multiple times. But Arnold does have a point because, for one, you have mentioned that you have no family and no children. And you being a senior at seventy-eight years old, you're not going to be able to continue living on your own for much longer. Thus, Arnold will have ownership of your house and you'll be sent to live in a nursing home."

"No! No please, anything but that! I've lived for fifty-three years in that house with my husband. Don't do this to me!" Mrs. Lopez said, being escorted out of the courtroom by her lawyer.

Heartbroken by the result of the trial, Connor felt some bitterness toward the judge. *How could she be so heartless? Mrs. Lopez looked like a healthy and strong woman, despite her age. I can't understand why she chose to give ownership to that smug-looking jerk.* Regardless, he couldn't do anything for Lopez and had to disregard it, focusing back on their case.

Once most of the people had left the courtroom, Chief Willie approached a woman at the plaintiff's table. Connor saw Chief Willie greet the woman with a handshake and whispered something into her ear. Connor found the whisper to be ambiguous but dismissed it as Chief Willie began to introduce them to the woman.

"Connor, Jim, this is Nancy Adams. She's the city's District Attorney and will be helping us on our case against Mr. Dixon," Chief Willie explained.

"It's a pleasure to meet you both," said Nancy, shaking both Connor and Jim's hands.

"The pleasure is ours. So, what can we do to take down Mr. Dixon?" Jim asked.

"Well, first James proposed we get a search warrant for Mr. Dixon. But I believe an arrest warrant works better here. Because for one, the evidence for his arrest is already substantially stronger than being able to search his properties. And once he's arrested you could do an interrogation to potentially find out the identity of The Mortem," Nancy explained.

"Wow, I guess that settles it. Let's go get this warrant!" Connor said, thrilled.

"Yes, but I'm going to need the judge's signature for the warrant, and the judge has already left to go home. She does a trial once per day, so I'll have to ask her tomorrow when she's free. In the meantime, you guys should try taking a break yourselves," Nancy said, leaving the courtroom.

Hearing what Nancy said, Connor's eyebrows lifted at the realization. *I can't believe it... It's been so long since I or Jim have taken a genuine break.* Turning to Jim, he knew that Jim deserved a break more than anyone.

"Hey, chief, you know where we could all go to relax?" Connor asked.

"Hmm, there is this one place where my mother and I love to go to," Chief Willie replied.

Afterward, they drove to a venue where Connor and Jim could see a crowd of people standing outside. Parking their cars along the roadside, Connor wondered where Chief Willie was taking them. Upon entering the venue, they were in what looked like a theater with a stage and jazz musicians performing live.

"Wow, I've never been to a jazz club before," Connor remarked.

"I think I've been to one of these once when I was in my thirties. I gotta say, nothing is more lovely than to unwind at a club, especially one with live music," Jim said as they all sat down at a table.

"… So, chief, you mentioned that you and your mother love to come here?" Connor asked.

"That's right, but the main reason my mother loves these jazz clubs is because she plays the saxophone. Jazz is her passion and like mother, like son, jazz is also my passion. Though, I can't play any instrument, let alone the saxophone."

"You and your mom sound like you're really close… Must be nice to still have your parents with you," Connor said, tearing up.

"… Hey, how about we go and get a drink at the bar. It'll be on me," Chief Willie said.

"Hmm, alright, but I don't drink alcohol, but a club soda would be nice," Connor said as the three walked over to a bar counter.

When the three of them took a seat at the bar counter, Chief Willie ordered two shots of tequila and a club soda. Meanwhile, Connor contemplated the night that was Sterling's party. *What exactly was that deal Sterling had with Mr. Dixon? Was The Mortem present at the party, but slipped away during Mr. Dixon's arrival?* Despite the numerous thoughts running through his mind, he was brought back to reality when the bartender handed each of them their drinks.

"I remember back in my youth that I was able to drink ten shots… But now in my late fifties, I can only manage two," said Chief Willie drinking his shot.

"Heh, really? Well, I may not be a liquor expert, but I've seen Jim being able to drink twenty shots of tequila!" Connor said, sipping his club soda.

"Is that true? You're really able to drink 'twenty' shots? If so, you are one of a kind, sir," Chief Willie said, patting Jim on the back.

"Well, I prefer not to brag, but I have been able to drink as many as twenty or twenty-five shots. Though usually if I go more than twenty, I black out… I've been told I have strong kidneys, but I've been trying to give up alcohol lately," Jim said, drinking his shot of tequila.

"… Well, anyway, it's getting late, so I guess I'll see you both tomorrow. I'm sure in the morning, Nancy will have the judge's signature for the arrest warrant. So, be ready when we arrest Mr. Dixon," Chief Willie said, leaving the jazz club.

When morning came, Connor and Jim received a phone call from Chief Willie saying to meet him at Mr. Dixon's casino, The Royal Chalice. Making their way to The Royal Chalice, both of their eyebrows lifted when they saw that the streets of downtown central looked different from the west of downtown. The streets were spotless, with little to no trash, and had countless shops that were crowded with people. However, once they reached the casino, all of that became irrelevant.

When they arrived, Connor and Jim's eyes widened, seeing how massive the building was. Nonetheless, they turned their attention to the numerous police cars parked at the entrance of the casino. Exiting the car, they saw Chief Willie and his many officers restraining Mr. Dixon until they finally managed to handcuff him.

"Mr. Dixon, you have the right to remain silent. Anything you say can and will be used against you in a court of law. You have the right to an attorney. If you cannot afford an attorney, one will be provided for you. Do you understand the rights I have read to you?" Chief Willie said, stating the Miranda Warning.

"Yes, officer…"

As Mr. Dixon was seated inside a police car, Mr. Dixon caught a glimpse of Connor. Staring at Connor, Mr. Dixon gave off a bloodthirsty glare, as if he wanted to tear him apart. Connor noticed Mr. Dixon's glare, and it sent shivers down his spine, seeing that Mr. Dixon wouldn't take his eyes off him.

It was only until Mr. Dixon was driven away, by two officers. Taking a breath of relief, Connor sighed, knowing Mr. Dixon no longer had his sight on him. Thinking they'd won, Connor looked up, admiring the casino building.

Now at the police station, Connor and Jim prepared themselves before entering the interrogation room. Taking deep breaths, Connor thought about his theory, wondering whether it could be true. When it was time for the interrogation, Chief Willie arrived along with two other officers.

"Alright, as you both enter the interrogation room, me and these other officers will be here watching the interrogation through a one-way mirror."

"Got it, and you'll be able to hear us too?" Connor asked.

"Every word," Chief Willie replied.

Entering the interrogation room, the two came face to face with Mr. Dixon. Sitting across from Mr. Dixon, Connor received that same menacing glare from before. However, before Connor spoke, he took a deep breath.

"Do you remember me?" Connor asked.

"Remember you? How could I forget you? You're the one who punched me!" Mr. Dixon shouted, trying to break free from his cuffs.

"Alrighty then, how about we get started? Can you tell me what you know about The Mortem?"

"What? What is a Mortem?"

"Don't you play dumb with us! We know you're the one employing The Mortem! You hired him to murder the mayor and his wife, along with numerous other government officials throughout the country. Just admit it!" Connor shouted, standing up from his chair.

"I don't know what you're insinuating, but I swear to my late father that I don't know anything about this *Mortem*. Though, if this Mortem has been going on a killing spree, murdering countless government officials. Then this fella sounds like someone I'd like to be friends with, haha!"

Clenching his fist, Connor's breathing became heavier by the second. This led to Jim having to pull Connor away. Patting Connor's back, Jim said the following.

"I know you're frustrated Connor, but you need to be smart when you interrogate someone. Don't let them get to you and you got to remember to stay focused."

Nodding, Connor responded, "I know… I'm sorry Jim. I don't know what got over me. Alright, how about you take a turn in the interrogation?"

Now sitting down, Jim proceeded and said, "I apologize for Connor's aggressiveness, Mr. Dixon, but we're only here to find answers… Okay so, this journal was found in the apartment of Briana Harper. She was a journalist investigating the rumors of The Mortem killings and was finding connections to *your* casino. She claimed in her notes that you've been conducting human trafficking. Can you confirm to me whether this is true or not?" Jim said, showing Mr. Dixon the pages of Briana's journal.

With a blank expression, Mr. Dixon looked Jim in the eyes and responded, "… No, I would *never* commit any sort of crimes against humanity. My casino is just that, a place where the public can gamble."

"Oh really? Well, in that case, was this not you?" Jim said, showing a photo of Mr. Dixon, smoking a cigar while in the background showing several tied-up women being loaded into a trailer of a semi-truck.

Without uttering a word Mr. Dixon's eyes widened at the photo, which led Jim to chuckle, "Your reaction is *all* the proof I needed. Alright, we're done here."

Afterward, as the two left the interrogation room they met up with Chief Willie, who had been watching the interrogation from the one-way mirror. Chief Willie applauded both and beckoned one of his officers to come. The officer came and handed us both a cup of coffee.

"What's with the coffee?" Jim asked.

"Oh, you can think of it as a thank you for everything you both have done. Anyways, Jim, there's something I'd like to talk to you about. Could you come with me? It'll only take a minute," Chief Willie asked, glancing at Jim's trench coat.

"Oh, sure. But what is it you want to talk to me about?"

"I just want to discuss something with you."

"Hmm, okay. Connor, could you wait for me outside? I won't be long."

"Alright, I'll see you in a bit then," Connor said as Jim and Chief Willie made their way into another room.

As Connor exited the police station, he stood outside and watched the cars driving down the road. Following this, he began contemplating how far they'd come since they accepted Chief Willie's case. A part of him, however, wondered what would have happened if they decided not to accept Chief Willie's case. Nevertheless, they were still not finished with the case and needed to find out the identity of The Mortem. However, there were still a few things that puzzled him. *Why didn't Sterling tell me the details of the deal he made with Mr. Dixon? Could Sterling's deal have something to do with Mr. Dixon's human trafficking?* Holding his chin, he thought about everything that had happened, but as he did, he'd be approached by Nancy.

"Hello, Connor, I was just told by James that you and Jim have finished interrogating Mr. Dixon," Nancy said as she stood next to Connor.

"Oh, yeah, we just did. Though we weren't able to get Mr. Dixon to confess to anything. But Jim did manage to get a reaction from Mr. Dixon by showing him a photo. His reaction may not count as a confession, but it did confirm to us that he's guilty of something."

"I see, and this photo… What's the context of it?"

"The photo? Well, I didn't get much of a good look at it, but basically, it was a photo of Mr. Dixon being caught in the act of human trafficking. We found the photo inside a journal that belonged to this journalist Briana Harper… who we found dead in her apartment."

"My goodness, that's horrible. I swear that Mr. Dixon will be going behind bars. I'll do everything in my power to prosecute him… Anyway, I must get going, but it was nice talking to you. Oh, and just so you know, the trial for Mr. Dixon is scheduled to take place a few days from now. So, I'll see you around… detective."

On the day of the trial, Connor entered the police station. Once inside, he went to the jail cells where he found Mr. Dixon sitting inside his cell. He saw that Mr. Dixon was conversing with his lawyer, who was sitting in a chair outside the cell. When Mr. Dixon's lawyer saw him, he whispered something to Mr. Dixon before leaving. Once Mr. Dixon's lawyer left, Connor went and sat on the same chair.

"What brings you here? You've come to mock me?" Mr. Dixon said, in shackles.

"Something like that… But I just want to know something. That deal you had with Sterling. What exactly was the deal you both had? Sterling told me that he ended the previous deal due to you wanting more money. Is that true?" Connor clarified.

"Is this some kind of joke? You *people* think you own the world, but that's where you're wrong! This world is run by the strong who rule over the weak, and I am not weak!"

"What on earth are you talking about?"

"Haha, you're good, you almost make it seem like you're not one of them. But I won't be fooled!"

"Okay that's it, you're insane! I hope you get used to living in a cell because that's where you'll be spending the rest of your miserable life in!" Connor exclaimed, leaving the jail.

Storming out of the jail, Connor contemplated what Mr. Dixon said to him. *Why did Mr. Dixon believe that he was being fooled? What was he even talking about?* Connor knew that things weren't adding up. Nonetheless, it didn't change the fact that Mr. Dixon was a disgusting psychopath.

Now as he stood in the police station, he was greeted by Chief Willie, "Hello Connor, what are you doing here? Shouldn't you be at the courthouse with Jim?"

"Yeah, I should but I wanted to ask Mr. Dixon something before his trial starts," Connor replied.

"Oh really? And what would that be?"

"... Well, I didn't even get an ordinary response from him. I don't know, it was weird, he said that I almost made it seem like I wasn't one of them... Who's them?"

"... I see, you know when it comes to questioning prisoners. You can't always believe what they say. Sometimes, they say things just to confuse you."

"Right, you're right. I can't let Mr. Dixon get to my head. I got to stay focused... Okay then, I guess I'll see you at the courthouse," Connor said, leaving the police station.

Arriving at the courthouse, Connor saw the press blocking the entrance. Trying to reach the entrance, he made his way through the press. Despite the feeling of being crushed, he managed to enter the courthouse and was then greeted by Jim.

"There you are, Connor. Where were you?" Jim asked.

"Sorry, I just wanted to do something before the trial started... But it wasn't even worth my time," Connor explained.

"I see. Well, the trial is about to start soon so let's go sit down," Jim said, leading him to the courtroom.

Entering the courtroom, they both sat in the public seating area. Glancing around the courtroom, Connor saw the jury getting into their seats. He also caught a glimpse of Nancy, who was entering the courtroom. At that moment, he remembered they needed to give Briana's journal to Nancy.

"Jim, where's Briana's Journal? We need to give it to Nancy so she can present it as evidence," Connor asked.

"Oh, I have it right here. Let me just… That's strange, it's gone," said Jim searching his trench coat.

"What do you mean it's gone? Where is it?"

"Well, the last time I saw it was when we finished interrogating Mr. Dixon a few days ago. I always thought I just left it in my trench coat, but it's not here."

"Jim, if we don't have that journal, we can't charge Mr. Dixon with human trafficking. Though, we could still charge him with assault and attempted murder… But it won't be enough to give him a life sentence."

Following that, the courtroom fell into a deep silence once Mr. Dixon arrived. Connor watched as Mr. Dixon was escorted by an officer to the defendant's table. Soon after, Mr. Dixon's lawyer sat next to Mr. Dixon, who was still handcuffed. Once everyone had sat down, the bailiff raised his voice and stated the following.

"All rise, the court is now in session. The honorable judge Amber Carson is presiding. The People vs. Frederick Dixon," proclaimed the bailiff.

"Be seated… Ladies and gentlemen of the jury, the defendant has been charged with numerous serious crimes and will be innocent until proven guilty. Now then, Ms. Adams, are the people ready to begin opening statements?" the Judge declared openly.

"Yes, your honor… Members of the jury, on the night that was Charles Sterling's party that was commemorating Mayor Johnson's death, Mr. Dixon *along with his men* not only broke into Sterling's manor but threatened the very lives of the guests of said party. And when Mr. Dixon was eventually confronted by Sterling, you know what he did? He shot him point blank in the shoulder… Nearly taking his life. It is a miracle that Sterling survived, but just imagine if paramedics had not arrived in time… this would have been a murder case. And for that, this man is guilty," said Nancy, reciting her opening statement.

"Thank you, Ms. Adams, you may now take a seat. Mr. Santiago, will you begin your opening statement?"

"Why yes, your honor… Members of the jury and *madam judge*, Mr. Dixon may come off to you at first as a heinous criminal that deserves to be sent to prison. However, if you find it in your heart to look past that, what you'll see is a man… A man who retains his pride and his dignity. There is no hiding the fact that Mr. Dixon is not perfect… because the truth is that no one is perfect, and everyone makes mistakes. Which is why I conclude that Mr. Dixon is innocent," said Mr. Santiago, reciting his opening statement.

"I see, well done Mr. Santiago, you may now take a seat. Alright then, Ms. Adams, are you ready to bring in your first witness?"

"Of course, your honor. Allow me to bring him in," Nancy said, beckoning Connor to come sit on the witness stand.

When Connor sat on the witness stand, he could feel multiple eyes looking at him. With his hands shaking, he felt like he was put under a spotlight on stage and had to speak in front of a large crowd. Following that, Nancy cleared her throat. As she stood before Connor, she began to question him.

"Mr. Davis is it true that Mr. Dixon and his men threatened Sterling and all the guests that were at Sterling's party?" asked Nancy.

"Yes, it's true. They terrorized everyone at that party," Connor responded.

"I see. And is it true that you were assaulted by Mr. Dixon himself? Not to mention nearly choked to death by him?"

"Yes… It was horrible, I felt like I couldn't breathe and at the same time could feel the weight of Mr. Dixon on me. I couldn't move at all," Connor explained.

Once Connor answered all the questions, the judge instructed Connor to leave the witness stand. Right when he was about to comply, he hesitated. Pausing in his action, he realized something that triggered an immediate response from him.

"Wait! I'm not done yet. There's still one thing we haven't accused Mr. Dixon of. And that's his disgusting human trafficking crimes!" Connor shouted, pointing at Mr. Dixon.

"Oh, I see… And do you have proof of this Mr. Davis?" the Judge asked.

"We do! It was all in a journal we found! But we… lost it."

"Forgive me Mr. Davis, but without proof, your claims are merely hearsay and are irrelevant to the claims already made to the accused. Now then, would you please leave the witness stand?"

Feeling like all he did was pointless; Connor grudgingly left the witness stand and exited the courtroom. Seeing this, Jim also left the courtroom and proceeded to follow him. Clenching his jaw, he ran to a wall and kicked it. Soon after, his left shoulder was grabbed by Jim, who pulled him away from the wall.

"Hey, what do you think you're doing? Come on, tell me what's wrong," Jim said.

"I'm sorry Jim but if we just had that journal. We could have sent that bastard away for years… Are you sure that you didn't just leave the journal at the hotel?"

"I'm really sorry Connor, but I swear I don't know where the journal is. Though, when we finished interrogating Mr. Dixon, I was talked to by Chief Willie. I think I remember leaving the journal on a counter nearby, but I can't remember if I picked it back up… You don't think Chief Willie would have taken it, do you?"

"What? No, Chief Willie wouldn't sabotage our own evidence. That's ridiculous… He wouldn't do that."

Standing in the hallways of the courthouse, they heard the doors of the courtroom open. When they turned around to see who had left, a sudden chill ran down both their spines. Paralyzed, Connor watched as Mr. Dixon walked past them, no longer cuffed. Feeling tightness in his chest, Connor ran back into the courtroom and confronted the judge.

"Judge! Can you explain to me why on earth is Mr. Dixon walking down the hallway a free man?" Connor shouted.

"Hmm? Oh, well he paid his bail. Since he was prosecuted for attempted murder and assault, I gave him bail of five hundred thousand dollars. And once he paid the bail, he became a free man," the Judge replied while she counted stacks of cash.

"What? Why would you even give him bail? He almost murdered Sterling and *everyone* at that party!"

Clenching his fists, Connor glared at the judge, but he soon came back to his senses when Jim placed his hand on his shoulder. Glancing at Jim, he took a deep breath and stepped away from the judge. With a frown on his face, he stormed out of the courthouse, leaving without Jim.

An hour later, Connor walked the streets of downtown, contemplating what to do next. *I know if we just had proof that Mr. Dixon was conducting human trafficking then we could finally take him down… But getting proof was easier said than done.* Eventually, as he strolled down the sidewalk, he caught sight of the city's hospital.

Entering the hospital, Connor went up the elevator and walked down the hallway. He looked around each door for the room number that Sterling was staying in. Once he found the room door, he knocked a couple of times until he heard Sterling.

"Come inside, the door is unlocked."

When entering Sterling's room, Connor saw floating balloons tied to a chair. There were also a couple of gifts on a table next to Sterling. Sterling was lying in bed and was wearing a hospital gown.

"Connor, thank you for visiting. How have you been? I heard from James that you all took old Dixon to court… How did it go?" Sterling asked.

"Yeah, umm about that. Mr. Dixon did lose the case, but the judge gave him a bail of five hundred thousand dollars. Which he paid and was given back his freedom," Connor explained, sitting in a chair.

"I see, and does this bother you?"

"Bother me? I mean, yeah it does bother me because there was no justice dealt in that trial… I'm sorry Sterling but… I don't know what to do," Connor said, clenching his head with both hands.

"Hmm, you know… whenever I'm stressing out about something, I'd always play some chess with a friend. Do you want to play a round?" Sterling said, taking out a chessboard and placing it on the table nearby.

"Chess huh? I guess one game wouldn't hurt."

Beginning their game, Sterling chose the white pieces and Connor chose the black pieces. With each taking their turn, they captured numerous pieces from the other. Minutes pass, and the two find themselves in a stalemate.

Tapping his finger on his leg, he contemplated his next move. He thought over whether he should capture one of Sterling's knights. But by doing so, he risked losing one of his bishops. However, before he could make his move, Sterling uttered something.

"A chess game is like a war on a board. With the goal to outsmart your opponent… Do you understand?" Sterling asked.

"Umm, I think so? I don't know, that kinda came out of nowhere," Connor replied.

"Heh, my apologies. I've always found chess to be… philosophical. But it's true, just like in real life, we're always fighting wars, trying to beat our opponents, whether that opponent is the hardships of work, poverty, and of course criminal justice.

After hearing what Sterling said, it sparked an idea in Connor. Contemplating his idea, Connor stood up and walked to the hospital room window. Looking out the window, he pondered his idea further until finally making his decision.

"I know what I'm going to do now… I need to call Jim and Chief Willie. I'm so sorry to leave so suddenly but maybe we could finish our game of chess another time?" Connor said, looking back at Sterling.

"Of course, you go and do what needs to be done."

"Alright then, thank you, Sterling, for everything. I'll see you soon!" Connor said, leaving Sterling's room.

"… A war on a board. Only time will tell who will checkmate the other first."

Chapter 5
The Royal Chalice

Later that night Connor waited for Jim and Chief Willie at an empty parking lot. While he waited for Jim and Chief Willie, he had some second thoughts about his idea. *Am I doing the right thing? This plan of mine is a little illegal and crazy, but what other options do we have?* Once Jim and Chief Willie arrived, he shook his head and walked up to them.

"Guys, I know this meeting was sort of out of the blue, but I think I've finally figured out how we can take down Mr. Dixon once and for all," Connor clarified.

"What? Connor, we lost Briana's journal. How are we going to accuse Mr. Dixon of something we don't have proof of anymore?" Jim inquired.

"I'll tell you how. Because if proof is what we need, then how about we go get it ourselves! I already thought of everything. We would all go undercover at Mr. Dixon's casino, take photos of what we see with these cameras I've bought, and get out. Simple as that... So, what do you say?" Connor said, showing them the cameras.

"But don't we need a warrant to even investigate Mr. Dixon's casino and his properties? I don't know Connor... maybe we should just give up," Jim said.

"Give up? Come on Jim, don't be like that... If we do this, just imagine the number of *lives* we could save. Chief, you agree with me, right?"

"... Hmm, yes, this could work. Even though it's very risky and illegal without a warrant, we should at least try taking down this bastard one last time. I could even convince the judge to accept the proof that we will obtain," Chief Willie said, taking a brief glance at the cameras Connor bought.

"What? You're agreeing to this? Okay fine, but if we're going to do this, promise me that you won't do anything reckless."

"I promise Jim... You have my word. Now then, it's time for us to expose this so-called kingpin."

As the three headed to The Royal Chalice, they parked along the roadside near the casino. Once they were dressed in different clothing, they'd make their way to the casino. Reaching the casino, they noticed how the exterior of the casino was almost entirely lit up by neon lights and was jammed with people inside.

Entering the casino, they found themselves in an area crammed with slot machines. The area's floor was also carpeted red, and it was adorned with a golden artistic pattern. With pop music playing in the background, they proceeded with their investigation.

Splitting up, they each went to investigate a different area, with Connor staying in the area with slot machines. As he explored the area, he looked for anything suspicious. However, it turned out that everything looked suspicious when considering that he was at a casino. After half an hour of investigating, he still found no leads.

Arriving at a bar counter, Connor sat down on a chair and ordered a club soda. While the bartender prepared his club soda, he overheard a group of men at a poker table nearby. At first, he dismissed them, but he then had an odd suspicion about the group.

As a result, Connor glanced at the group of men and realized that something about them looked familiar. At that point, he recognized they were the same men who had acted as bodyguards for Mr. Dixon at Sterling's party. Not wanting to blow his cover, he kept his head down and attempted to listen in on what the group of men were saying.

"Son of a bitch! I lost again!" one of the men shouted.

"Hey, it's not my fault you suck at poker. We've played seven times already, you must be broke by now," the other man said, counting stacks of cash.

"… No, one more round!" the man said, placing another stack of cash on the poker table.

Meanwhile, another one of the men took out a cigarette and tried lighting it. However, the man suddenly received a phone call and when the man answered the call, his eyes widened. He thus snapped his fingers vigorously at the group, in effect silencing them, and began talking on the phone.

"Sir, how can we help you? … Yes, we can do that, and would you like us to do anything else? … Alright, we will be there soon," said the man, hanging up.

"Was it the boss?" one of the men asked.

"Yeah, and he said that we need to load the cargo for the truck. So, let's not keep him waiting."

Still having his head down, Connor watched the group of men clear out from the poker table. He pursued the group of men but kept a distance from them. Eventually, he saw the group of men enter a VIP lounge using a keycard.

After this, Connor informed Jim and Chief Willie of what he'd uncovered. Now, with the three back together, they tried to devise a plan to enter the VIP lounge. They came up with a few ideas to get inside, but they suddenly noticed the doorknob of the VIP lounge turning, which caused them to merge with the crowd nearby. Glancing back at the VIP lounge door, they saw a tattooed man exit the door. Connor recognized this man as one of the men from before. As he watched the man, he noticed the man putting a keycard in his left back pocket.

"If we wanna get in, we need that keycard," Chief Willie said.

"Yeah, but we can't steal it. Isn't that against the law?"

"Connor, sometimes when it comes to working on a case, we must get our hands dirty from time to time. It's okay, we're doing this for the greater good, remember that," Chief Willie explained.

"I guess… Alright, I'm on it."

Following the man, Connor saw the man return to the poker table. He saw that the man was digging through the mess made by the group. He attempted to swipe the keycard but failed to do so when the man turned around. As a result, the man managed to walk away but was suddenly approached by Jim who confronted the man.

"Hello there, I was just passing by and noticed that you were looking for something. Do you need any help?" Jim asked the man and winked at Connor.

"Uh, no, I found what I was looking for already, but thank you anyway. It's funny, I completely forgot to bring the money I won from playing seven rounds of poker," the man said, oblivious to Connor swiping the keycard from him.

Afterward, the three finally used the keycard and were able to infiltrate the VIP lounge. Now, having entered the VIP lounge, to their surprise, it was vacant, with no one in sight. When searching the lounge, Jim checked several drawers of cabinets, which mostly comprised a variety of glass wine bottles. Chief Willie on the other hand checked under the club chairs and found a bag that contained a white powder that was taped beneath the chair.

Meanwhile, Connor looked around the lounge and came across a dove figurine. The figurine was white and stood on top of a wooden lamp table. The figurine looked strange to him, considering it looked out of place in the drug and alcohol-ridden room. Inspecting the figurine, he felt a button underneath the wooden lamp table.

When Connor pressed the button, a hidden door within the walls opened. Gazing inside the hidden door, he discovered it to be an elevator. Examining the elevator, he noticed how it had stains of what he could assume to be blood. However, as he was checking the elevator, he was approached by Jim.

"Hey, umm, can we talk?" Jim asked, stuttering.

"Oh, sure, what is it?" Connor replied.

"Well, I was just thinking... that maybe you were right back then. That we shouldn't do this case."

"Wait, what? You want to quit? Now, after we've come so far?"

"I'm sorry Connor but this has become too much for me... And I think you should quit as well because *this* has become an obsession. You may not admit it, but the reason you become so fixated on solving a case is because you don't want to think about what happened three years ago. They are dead Connor; you need to stop living in the past!"

"... You shut your mouth right now. They weren't even your family... You just happened to be an old friend of my dad! But you don't know what it's like, to lose your entire family in one *fucking* night! You want to quit so badly? Well, go right ahead, I don't need you!"

As Jim's eyes widened seeing Connor's reaction, Jim took a deep breath and proceeded to the door. Taking one last look at Connor, Jim stepped out of the VIP lounge. Once Jim was gone, Connor realized what he had done and began regretting it. A sense of guilt soon consumed him as he was about to go back and apologize to Jim, but Chief Willie stood in his way.

"Jim has made his choice. If he wants to quit then let him," Chief Willie explained.

"But I need to apologize for everything I said to him... Maybe he'll change his mind?" Connor said.

"Maybe, but it's better if we continue without him. He'd just slow us down anyway."

Having to decide whether to pursue Jim or carry on without him caused Connor to become conflicted. In the end, Chief Willie's words convinced Connor to proceed. Now entering the elevator, Connor and Chief Willie discovered that the elevator had two buttons with numbers one and two. The button with the number one lit up, suggesting they were on the first level. Thus, they pressed the button with the number two.

After pressing the button, the elevator descended, taking them under the casino. Before the elevator door opened, Chief Willie pulled out his pistol and took cover. Connor did the same and when they finally arrived, they found themselves at an underground facility. As the two gradually walked across the empty hallway of the facility, they eventually reached an ominous red door.

Approaching the red door, Connor could hear hip-hop music playing, and when he pressed his ear against the door, he tried listening to the other side.

Eavesdropping through the door, he heard a man proclaiming people's bids that spanned from ten to a hundred thousand dollars. After hearing several people's bids, Connor opened the door and inspected the room inside. The room was packed with old men sitting in green club chairs and had a woman on a stage, dressed in a blue bikini.

Feeling revolted by the sight, Connor clenched his fist firmly. His breathing also became heavier as he glared at all the old men placing their bids. This got the attention of Chief Willie, who grabbed onto Connor's shoulder.

"Connor, I need you to calm down or else you'll blow our cover," Chief Willie whispered, holding onto Connor's shoulder.

"I can take them; I can take all of them. We need to save her!" Connor said, clenching his jaw.

"We can't help her right now! The only thing we can do is take some photos as evidence. Remember why we're here. Don't worry, once we have enough evidence, we will track down everyone that bastard Mr. Dixon has sold, and we'll reunite them with their families."

"… You're right, we got to stick to the plan… but it still feels wrong, doing nothing."

"We're not doing *nothing*, what we're doing is what will allow us to shut this entire place down."

"Yeah… You're right," Connor said, taking a photo of the auction room.

Following that, the two continued to traverse through the facility's hallways, trying not to be caught on camera. Towards the end of the facility, they found themselves in a hallway with cell doors on both sides of the walls. Traveling across the hallway, it echoed with whimpering.

As they proceeded along the hallway, Connor's heart plummeted when he witnessed children held captive in cells. A tear came down from his eye as he saw the innocent children forced to live in inhuman conditions. Knowing he could not help those crying, he swallowed his frustration and tried to remain calm as he continued taking photos for evidence.

"Hey, I know you feel helpless, but *we* cannot do anything for them right now. Put aside what is happening right now and focus on what can happen. That being us shutting down this place for good. But for that to happen, we need to keep moving."

"I know, but *this* is becoming too much for me… I don't know, maybe Jim was right… We shouldn't have come down here."

"Connor, look at me… We are these poor souls' last hope. Think about them, think about Sterling and all the people The Mortem has killed."

"… You're right, I can't give up. Especially since we're so close."

"Good, now let's keep going."

When they reached the end of the facility, they were outside and saw some men loading a semi-truck. Observing the men loading the semi-truck trailer, Connor noticed something familiar. He recognized that the men loading the trailer were the same men he saw back at the poker table.

Taking a closer look, Connor's eyes widened, realizing what he was looking at. It turned out that the cargo were children held in cages. His jaw dropped, not wanting to believe his eyes. Unable to turn his gaze away, all he could do was watch.

"Hey Nicolas, where's Joseph? He's supposed to be helping me load these brats," one of the men said, loading the children into the semi-truck's trailer.

"He said he forgot something at the poker table. He's probably on his way right now. But just because he isn't here doesn't give you an excuse to slack off. So, get back to work!"

Meanwhile, Connor stood there frozen and still couldn't believe his eyes. The sight of the group of men loading children as if they were merchandise made him nauseous. Just as Connor was about to take more photos, Chief Willie interrupted him.

"Connor, I found a surveillance room. There could be stronger evidence that we can gather there," Chief Willie said, whispering to Connor.

From Chief Willie to the children being shipped, he contemplated whether he should try to save the children or continue to follow Chief Willie. *What should I do? While we could potentially save thousands of lives with the evidence, does that mean I should just ignore these children?* Although he was torn between the two, he ultimately nodded at Chief Willie.

Making their way inside the surveillance room, Connor and Chief Willie inspected the space. While they searched the room, Connor felt a feeling of guilt that was eating away at his chest. He regretted abandoning the children, but he looked at Chief Willie and remembered why he chose to do it.

Eventually, they found the surveillance officer who was snacking on some chips. They tried to figure out how to get past the surveillance officer. But the officer suddenly caught a glimpse of something on the monitors. With the surveillance officer distracted Connor tackled the surveillance officer. Restraining the surveillance officer, Chief Willie was able to knock out the surveillance officer with his baton.

Standing guard, Chief Willie watched if anyone entered the surveillance room. Meanwhile, Connor browsed through the security footage, fast-forwarding through hours of footage. With each piece of footage Connor watched, his heart pounded, seeing everything horrible that had taken place in the facility. Following that, Connor tried choosing which footage they should use as evidence against Mr. Dixon. But when he was doing this, something *unusual* caught his eye.

Observing the footage on the monitor, he saw what appeared to be a meeting taking place. The meeting was held three months ago. And as he watched the footage, he saw Mr. Dixon and his bodyguards welcoming a group of people in black cloaks who also wore matching white masks. In the footage, Mr. Dixon invited the group of masked people to sit at a round boardroom table. Goosebumps soon covered his body, watching this unfold. However, a chill ran down his spine once he saw the unspeakable.

His reality soon came crumbling down when the group of masked people began removing their masks. Several of those who removed their masks he recognized were some of the guests from Sterling's party. He also recognized some as officers that he recalled from the police station. However, his eyes widened when one of them turned out to be Chief Willie.

As he lay paralyzed, his heart sank when he heard a gun cocked behind him. Raising his hands, he gradually turned around to see Chief Willie aiming his pistol at him. Not knowing what to do, he watched in horror, seeing Chief Willie becoming unrecognizable.

"I didn't want you to find out like this... I really didn't, but you and Jim have become a problem that I have to solve," Chief Willie said.

"Wait, I don't understand... You were involved in this?"

"Yes, I know it must come as a shock, but this is who I am... Who I always was. Though, if not for you and Jim, I wouldn't have been able to sneak in here. For that, I am grateful."

"I can't believe it... All this time, I thought—"

"Well, you thought wrong!" Chief Willie shouted, knocking out Connor with his baton.

When Connor regained consciousness, he eventually caught a glimpse of Chief Willie and saw him throw their cameras to the floor. Feeling like he was in a nightmare; he couldn't believe what was happening. Confirming his disbelief, he saw Chief Willie pull out Briana's journal and threw it on the floor. Pulling out a hip flask, Chief Willie began drenching the file cabinets and security monitors with alcohol.

Realizing he was handcuffed, he attempted to stand up, but Chief Willie confronted him. Looking down at him, Chief Willie chuckled, taking out a box of matches. After lighting a match, Chief Willie looked in awe at its flame.

"You know, it's a shame Jim couldn't be here with us. It would've made this so much easier. Killing two birds with one stone... But I guess I'll have to send some of my officers to visit him at the hotel room I got for the two of you."

"No, you can't! Please, chief, you don't have to do this. It's not too late."

"I'm afraid it is… But don't worry, you said you were Catholic, right? Well, lucky for you, you'll soon get to meet your God," Chief Willie said, throwing the lit match onto the security monitors and setting the surveillance room on fire.

Before leaving, Chief Willie took one last glance at Connor and nodded at him. Once Chief Willie fled the burning surveillance room, he tried standing up, but the flames grew as the fire spread. With the fumes contaminating the air, he began coughing as smoke filled the room. However, before he reached the exit, he heard the surveillance officer coughing, still unconscious. Even though he didn't want to, he knew that he couldn't just leave the man to die. Thus, he clutched onto the surveillance officer's shirt and began dragging the surveillance officer behind him.

Having exited the surveillance room, Connor gasped for air and rested against a wall to catch his breath. However, his break soon ended when he started receiving gunfire. Although handcuffed, he ran as fast as he could, avoiding the gunfire shot at him. After several close calls, he managed to avoid the men shooting at him.

As Connor continued running, he came across a man walking out of a door. Shoving the man back into the door, he wrapped his handcuffs around the man's neck. Choking the man until the man fell unconscious. Having almost been burned and shot to death, he rested against a wall, where he eventually passed out.

Chapter 6
Meeting an Unlikely Friend

Waking up, Connor was convinced that he had woken up from a nightmare; though, after seeing where he was, his eyes widened. He found himself in a room that had a variety of laboratory equipment. There were also some crates stacked up against the wall. Inspecting one of the crates, he found it filled with leaves. Guessing the room's purpose, he knew he couldn't stay for long.

The first thing Connor did was barricade the door with the crates and search the room for anything that could help him with his handcuffs. Eventually, he found a wire cutter and tried to use it against the handcuffs. Though, it couldn't do anything to be able to cut the chain of the handcuffs. As a result, he snapped and threw the wire cutters across the room, hitting some of the laboratory equipment. After taking deep breaths, he walked over to retrieve the wire cutters, but when he went to pick them up, he found them next to a Bunsen burner.

Seeing the Bunsen burner and the wire cutter, an idea came into Connor's mind. By holding the chains of the handcuffs over the burner's flame, he heated them until they began to soften. While he did this, he heard two men conversing outside the room door. The two men tried to open the door but couldn't since he had already barricaded the door.

Time was running out as the two men began thrashing against the door. Once Connor felt that the chain had softened enough, he tried to cut it with the wire cutter. A smile soon emerged on his face once he was able to finally cut the chain. However, just as he was able to free himself, the two me. managed to kick the door down, entering the room. Though, their eyebrows lifted when they saw the room vacant.

In the moments before they entered the room, Connor was able to hide himself behind one of the crates. Despite managing to cut the chain of the handcuffs, he still had the actual cuffs. As the two men searched the room, he slowly raised his hand and turned the light switch off.

As a result, the two men gasped, and began frantically aiming their rifles. While they did this, Connor snuck behind one of the men and tackled him. The man tried to shake Connor off, who was trying to grab onto the man's rifle. This led to the man shooting at the floor, and as the stream of bullets continued, he eventually shot at the roof, ravaging the roof lights. Shattered glass then came down on them, causing the man to let go of the rifle's trigger, which fell on the floor.

Grabbing onto the man's shirt, Connor hurled him into the other man. Now that both men were immobilized, Connor exited the room and ran back towards the elevator. Upon finding the elevator, he sighed, but as soon as the elevator opened, his heart sank as three armed guards appeared.

Paralyzed, Connor watched as the three-armed guards approached him. Crouching down, he grudgingly raised his hands and when the guards reached him, one of them grabbed hold of his left arm.

However, that was when Connor tugged the guard down and smashed the guard's face on the floor. This resulted in gunfire from the two other guards, but he managed to evade it by throwing the guard he had knocked out at another guard. Grabbing onto one of the other guard's rifles, he throat-punched them, causing them to let go of their rifle.

With Connor now aiming the rifle at the last guard, the two were at a stalemate, with both aiming at the other. Remembering what Jim told him before, he knew he couldn't kill the guard.

"Drop the rifle!" Connor shouted.

"You first!" shouted the guard, still aiming his rifle at Connor.

"Listen to me, I don't want to kill you. Just please, drop the rifle and let me leave!" Connor said, hoping the guard would fall for his bluff.

Without saying a word, the guard smirked, while aiming his rifle. Assuming the guard had fallen for his bluff, he sighed. But his eyes widened when he saw the guard turn around and started shooting at the elevator controls.

With his only hope of escaping being destroyed, Connor began to tremble. It also wasn't long until more guards arrived behind him. Surrounded, he had lost all hope of escaping.

Closing his eyes, Connor took a deep breath, accepting his fate. It was only until the facility's lights suddenly went out that he raised an eyebrow. Looking around, he suddenly caught sight of a woman, emerging from the darkness. The woman tackled one of the guards and stabbed the guard multiple times in the stomach. After that, she pulled out a pistol and fired at the guard behind him.

"Hey, if you wanna live, follow me!" the woman shouted, reloading her pistol.

Despite hearing the woman's remark, Connor couldn't move his legs. However, the woman sighed and walked up to him having finished reloading her pistol. She began snapping her fingers in his face, resulting in him coming back to his senses.

"Hello? Come on, get out of la la land! We need to go!" the woman said, pulling Connor's arm.

Following the woman, the one thing that ran through Connor's mind was who the woman was. Eventually, the woman led him to a closet where they both hid. Catching their breaths, he glanced at the woman out of curiosity. He noticed the woman was wearing a yellow shirt and a black jacket. The woman also wore a gray hat and had reddish-brown hair.

"You okay there?" the woman asked, wiping the blood off her face with some paper towel that was on a shelf next to them.

"Uh, yeah... I'm just in shock, that's all," Connor replied.

"Aw, poor you. You must be tired after running for your life all night long."

"Oh, umm, yeah it has actually—" Connor said, but saw the woman pointing her pistol at him.

"Alright, I'll be the one asking the questions... got it? Now then, who the hell are you? And why were those guards trying to kill you?"

After Connor explained his situation, the woman shook her head and began to laugh. Connor's eyes widened, seeing her laugh with no regard for him. Just as he was about to speak, the woman pointed her pistol at his forehead.

"You actually think I'd believe a story as ridiculous as that? Lie to me again and I swear that I will put a bullet in skull!" the woman stated, pressing her pistol against Connor's forehead.

"I'm telling you the truth! Please, you have to believe me... Look, I'm literally wearing police handcuffs! Do you think I'm wearing these because I want to?"

"Okay so let me get this straight. What you're telling me is that you basically had the bright idea to come down here, and get proof to be able to prosecute Mr. Dixon for human trafficking? But *apparently*, the chief of police betrayed you, left you here to die, and was actually involved in said human trafficking the whole time... Damn, now that's some bad luck... Hmm, okay I'll believe you. But don't get any ideas about betraying me," the woman said, still pointing her pistol at Connor's forehead.

"No betrayal, you got it ma'am. But yeah, nothing tonight has gone my way. I still can't believe it... I don't want to believe it. I thought Chief Willie was my friend and I trusted him with my life... Oh no, Jim! He's going to have Jim killed! I need to warn him!"

"Wait what? Who's Jim?"

"I'm sorry, but I have to find a way out of here. Please, can you help me?"

"Help you? Hmm, alright… but only if you help me first. I'm looking for someone… someone very important to me. You help me find her, and I'll find us all a way out of here."

"It's a deal," Connor said, shaking hands with the woman.

Leaving the closet, the two made their way through the facility's hallways. Walking through the hallways, Connor noticed how the lights of the entire building were still off. With limited vision, he stayed alert of every noise he could hear.

Stopping at the end of the hallway, the woman pulled out a map from her jacket. Gazing at the map, Connor realized that it was a map of the facility and saw the surveillance room on the map. Seeing the map, he recalled when he and Chief Willie passed by a hallway where children were being held captive in cells.

"Hey, I think I know where you might be able to find this person you're looking for. I remember earlier, I passed this hallway with the chief. It was where they were keeping children in cells… It was awful," Connor said, showing Anna the hallway on the map.

"What? They're keeping children in cells? I can't believe these monsters… Alright, well that hallway isn't far from here. We better hurry though, before they fix the facility's power," the woman said as they proceeded forward.

Arriving in the hallway, the woman was speechless when she saw the poor children. Tears came down her face, seeing all the children. She ran up to one of the cells and began calling out a girl's name.

"Madison! Madison, are you here? Please Madison, answer me!"

While the woman cried out for Madison, Connor leaned against the wall, watching for any guards. Hearing the woman's desperate search for Madison made him imagine himself as the parents of all the children being held captive. *The pain of having your child kidnapped must be one of the worst feelings anyone could experience. And learning that they were being held in these cells must make it all the worse.* The woman, meanwhile, continued searching each cell. It was only until she noticed one girl who was wearing a pink hat.

"Hey girl, that hat you're wearing, where did you get it?" the woman asked.

"Umm, a nice girl gave it to me…" the girl wearing the pink hat replied, coughing.

"Alright, and where is this girl now?"

"The bad men… took her away."

"Okay, and can you tell me when they took her away?"

"Umm, I don't know… But it was a long time ago."

"I see… Well, thank you so much. This means a lot to me," the woman said, standing back up.

Right when the woman was about to leave, her arm was pulled by Connor. Having been stopped, the woman looked at Connor with one eyebrow raised. Standing his ground, he proceeded to say the following.

"We can't just leave and forget about these kids. They have families who are looking for them," Connor stated.

"I'm sorry, but there's nothing we can do for them. I also hate abandoning them, but how are we going to escape this place with a bunch of kids when we are barely surviving? Besides, I didn't come down here to save *every* kid that's being trafficked. I only came to save Madison… And that's the only kid that matters to me."

Knowing that the woman had a point, Connor frowned. Remembering that Chief Willie had said something similar to him made him clench his jaw. Nevertheless, he approached the children and crouched in front of them.

"Listen to me, kids. I know that you're all going to be saved from this nightmare. I don't know when, but I want you all to pray to God that everything will be better… Just don't lose your faith," Connor said, crossing himself.

Holding back tears, Connor stood up and took one last look at the children before leaving. As Connor and the woman continued onward, he despised the thought of abandoning those kids again. Meanwhile, the woman continued to follow the map, but looked back and briefly gazed at Connor.

"You shouldn't have done that," said the woman.

"Done what?" Connor replied.

"Give hope to those kids… Trust me, don't make promises you can't keep."

"It's not about making promises… It's about having faith. To have faith in God that everything will work out in the end."

"Oh really? Well, if God is *so* powerful then why did God allow those poor kids to get in that situation in the first place?"

"I may not know what God has planned for all of us, but this wasn't God's doing… It was the Devil who had meddled with the lives of those kids. It may seem cruel, but everything that happens, whether it be good or bad, is for a reason. So, try not to be so quick to blame God for everything because he loves all of us."

"… Hmm, well anyway, if we keep moving forward from here, there's an area of the facility that leads outside. I say we go there next and see what we can find."

Arriving at the area, Connor recognized it to be where he saw the men from the poker table loading children into a semi-truck. Though the semi-truck was gone, and the area was vacant. Inspecting the area, Connor and the woman searched for anything to help them find Madison. While they searched, Connor contemplated everything that had happened so far.

Now that Connor knew he couldn't trust Chief Willie, he pondered who else he couldn't trust. He first thought of the judge who gave Mr. Dixon bail. He then thought of Nancy, who was prying about the photo Jim showed Mr. Dixon. It all added up, but the idea of it all making sense sent chills down his spine as he realized he couldn't trust anyone. Trying to keep his composure, he exhaled with his mouth and inhaled through his nose. Yet this only led to a moment of breathlessness. Eventually, the woman noticed him trembling and went to pat him on the back.

"Connor, you alright? You look tense," the woman asked.

"Huh? Oh, I'm just thinking that's all…"

"I see… Hey, I'm sorry for what I said before. I'm just angry that all of this had to happen. I wish I could snap my fingers, and everything becomes fine again."

"Heh, yeah it would be nice if we could do that… But we need eventually face reality and make the most of it."

"Yeah… Anyway, let's get back to searching for clues. There should be something here that could help us."

Settling down, Connor glanced back at the woman. Considering that the woman was looking for a girl named Madison, he wondered what the woman's story was. Considering the woman's reserved nature, he tried to build up some confidence before asking her anything.

"Hey, can I ask you something?" Connor asked, stuttering.

"Hmm? Oh sure, what is it?" the woman replied.

"I don't mean to pry, but this Madison that you're looking for… How did she get kidnapped by these people?"

"… It was about a month ago. Our mom just died recently, and we had to become independent. Madison, my little sister, wanted to help me pay rent by getting a job. I told her no and well just like any child, she was stubborn. One day when I came back home from work, Madison was gone. I looked *everywhere* and spent hours searching for her. It was only until one of my neighbors told me that he saw Madison get taken by a group of men in a black van… I called the police, but they were no help… It was then that I took matters into my own hands. And well, here I am."

"That's horrible… I'm so sorry."

"It's fine. But it is horrible… I just want my little sister back. That's all I want," the woman said, tearing up.

Lowering his eyebrows, Connor started looking at the woman in a new light. After that, he continued looking around the area and that's when he noticed a clipboard on the floor. Picking it up, he discovered that it had a document with children's names and their photos. Showing the woman, the clipboard, the woman's eyebrows lifted.

"If they have documents with all the names of children, they are trafficking... then they must have a copy of the document of Madison! But that means we got to find out where they are keeping all the documents," said the woman, clutching onto the clipboard.

As they speculated about where to go next, suddenly they heard someone. Hiding behind the crates nearby, they both watched from afar. While they watched, a man walked out holding a rifle. Connor immediately recognized the man as he remembered that the man was the one who was giving orders to the group who were loading children onto the semi-truck.

His stomach churned as Connor saw the man slowly walk around the area. A frown spreading across his face, he considered tackling the man right away, but due to his carelessness, he had caused the crate that they were hiding behind to creak. As a result, it got the attention of the man who began approaching them. Just as the man was about to discover them, the man's two-way radio began to transmit.

This stopped the man as he proceeded to answer the transmission, "Yes? Of course, boss, we will find the intruders... Sir, please forgive us, this will never happen again... Okay, thank you, sir, I will inform you once we find the intruders."

After the man finished speaking on the radio, the man went and checked behind the crates. However, once the man checked the crates, there was no one. The man sighed as he slipped a cigarette into his mouth. Just as the man was about to light his cigarette, he heard footsteps behind him. When the man turned around, he was knocked out by Connor, who struck him with a metal pole.

Waking up, the man found it difficult to move. The man realized that his hands were tied up with duct tape. When the man looked up, he was met with the woman aiming her pistol at his face.

"Oh, you got to be kidding me," the man muttered.

"Believe it asshole! Now tell us where you guys keep all the documents on each shipment of children!" the woman shouted, slapping the man.

"Ha! Nicolas would never betray boss!" the man shouted.

"Really? We're speaking in the third person. Fine, be like that," the woman said, snatching the metal pole from Connor.

Striking Nicolas's right leg with the metal pole, Nicolas cried out in pain but still wouldn't talk. Thus, the woman struck Nicolas's leg again and again.

As she fell into a fit of rage, she eventually had her arm tugged by Connor. Connor pulled her away from Nicolas and proceeded to walk up to Nicolas.

"Alright, let's cut to the chase. My friend here is looking for her sister whom you guys happened to have sold already. I don't know how much longer I'll be able to keep her under control, but I suggest you start talking if you want to keep that leg of yours," Connor said.

"… Hmm, okay *fine*, I'll help you two. The office where we store the shipment documents is down the hall—" Nicolas said but got cut off by the woman.

"Oh, hell no! You're going to show us the way yourself!" the woman said pressing her pistol against the side of Nicolas's head.

"… Very well."

Thus, Nicolas grudgingly led the way to the office room to Connor and the woman. Following Nicolas, Connor began to contemplate their current situation. *This doesn't feel right… This Nicolas guy agreed to help us too easily. I got to keep my guard up and not let this guy out of my sight.* Arriving at the office door, Connor kept an eye on Nicolas, not knowing if they were being tricked. The woman, meanwhile, tried opening the office door, but she found it locked.

"Hey, the door is locked. You have the key to get in?" said the woman.

"Nope, I was never given one. Looks like you came down here for nothing after all," Nicolas said, laughing.

However, something about the door looked familiar when Connor saw it. He noticed it had the same type of lock as the VIP lounge. As a result, he took out the key card he had stolen before. When Nicolas saw him taking out the keycard, his expression turned blank.

"What? How do you have a keycard?" Nicolas asked.

"Well, I kind of swiped it from one of your men back at the casino," Connor said as he chuckled.

"So that's why Joseph never showed his ugly mug…" Nicolas mumbled.

By using the keycard, Connor was able to unlock the office door. Entering the office, Connor witnessed files scattered around the office with a filled trash can in the corner. The woman, on the other hand, inspected the office. She managed to find some filing cabinets that stood against the wall. While the woman searched through each drawer of the file cabinets, Connor stood watch over Nicolas.

As Connor glanced around the room, he caught a glimpse of a clock. The time on the clock was two in the morning, meaning it's been roughly three hours since he first arrived at the casino. Knowing how long he'd been there made him ponder if Jim was still alive.

Meanwhile, the woman who had been searching the file cabinets found something and informed Connor, "Hey, these documents are all in alphabetical order. Do you think you can help me find the kids that have their names beginning with the letter M?"

"Of course, let's see which one of these is for Madison," Connor said as they both began searching the file cabinets accordingly.

Eventually, Connor came across the name Madison Kennedy. Next to the name, there was a picture of a little girl. The girl's face somewhat resembled the woman. Hoping he found the correct document; he showed the woman the document.

"Oh my God… That's her, that's my Madison! Okay, it says here that she was sold to… What? She was sold to *the order?*" the woman said, snatching the document from Connor.

"The order? Now what does that mean? Is there an address?" Connor asked.

"Yeah, here's one. Now I'm one step closer to finding Madison… Thank you Connor, for everything."

"Nah, it's no big deal…" Connor replied, but suddenly heard a radio transmission.

Turning around, Connor and the woman saw Nicolas operating his two-way radio. Realizing he had been found out, Nicolas scurried toward the door. Connor, however, managed to tackle Nicolas to the floor. Despite Connor's effort, they were surrounded by guards as the door was opened.

"Haha! I told you! Nicolas would never betray boss!"

Chapter 7
A Painful Past

Now captured, Connor and the woman were escorted to a wooden door. Entering the door, they found themselves in a large room. The room had a round boardroom table, which Connor recognized from the surveillance footage. *This was the same room where Mr. Dixon had a meeting with that group of masked people. I wonder what other meetings were also held here.*

Being led to the elevator inside the room, Connor's hope of escaping was diminished by the second. Nevertheless, he still held hope as recited the Lord's Prayer under his breath. Eventually, the elevator brought them to the top floor of the casino. There they were met with a curtain wall through which they could view the scenery of the city.

The two were then put into a room and had their hands tied with rope. A grin spread across Nicolas's face as he walked up to Connor and spat on him. Connor, however, didn't react as he bit his tongue to remain calm. Nicolas frowned at Connor's lack of reaction, which resulted in Nicolas punching Connor's face.

In response to seeing Connor getting punched, the woman snapped and shouted, "You fucking bastard! You can't do this to us!"

As a result, Nicolas took out a knife and placed it near the woman's neck as he whispered to her, "Careful love… or we'll do something even worse to you."

"Hey, you leave her alone!" Connor shouted.

"Or what? Your hands are all tied up. There's *nothing* you can do!" Nicolas said, punching Connor in the stomach.

Being punched in the stomach, Connor dropped to his knees. Feeling an unbearable pain in his abdomen, he took deep breaths to distract himself from the pain. Attempting to get back up, Nicolas suddenly stepped on his head.

"Oh no, you're not getting back up! We're just getting started—" Nicolas said but got cut off by another guard who just entered the room.

"Hey Nicolas, the boss wants to talk to you," said the guard.

"What? Damn it, it was just getting good! Alright, the rest of you stay here and watch these two. I'll be back," Nicolas said, leaving the room.

Following this, Connor and the woman stood in silence with hope dwindling. Hoping his prayers would be answered, Connor tried to control his frantic breathing. The woman, on the other hand, kept trying to break free from the ropes. With no use in breaking free, the woman began to cry out.

"Why… Why did it have to end like this? Is this how… I'm going to die?" the woman said, tearing up.

"Hey, don't lose hope. We're going to survive this; I know we will."

"Forget what I said! I was so stupid for thinking I could find Madison on my own… Why are you so calm? Aren't you scared about what's going happen to us?"

"I am scared, but… I have faith in God that we *will* make it! You just need to believe."

"Believe? Heh, I used to be a believer once… Our family, we were all Baptist. We even went to church every Sunday. But after *everything* that's happened, I just… stopped believing. I didn't care anymore."

"Yeah, I know what it's like when you get to a point where it becomes hard to believe. In fact, there was a time… Where I almost stopped believing.

It all started on the day that my dad officially opened his investigation agency. I was twelve years old at the time while my little brother Michael was ten. Boxes were still scattered around the office which Michael and I sometimes sat on top of. However, Mom would always yell at us for sitting on the boxes since we might break something inside them.

I loved our mom, she sometimes even baked homemade brownies whenever we did well on a test at school. In those days, everything just seemed perfect. I thought that our family would always stay together, and nothing could ever tear us apart... but I couldn't have been more wrong.

Later that day, Jim arrived at the agency to congratulate Dad on his first day of business. At the time I didn't know Jim as well as I do now, so I never would've imagined how much he was going to mean to me. Both Michael and I were shy but our mom, as always, made us say hello to the guest.

"… Hello," said both Michael and me.

"Why hello there boys! My goodness, you two are getting tall!" Jim said as he chuckled.

"That's right, my boys are getting so big," our mom said, smiling.

When Dad went to greet Jim, they began talking about their time together in the Marines. That's right, my dad and Jim met when they were both serving in the Marines. They considered each other brothers after the many years they'd spent serving together. In fact, Dad saved Jim from a grenade when they were on a mission once. At least that's what my dad always bragged about.

However, while Dad and Jim were babbling, I noticed Mom suddenly began to cough. Still coughing, she went rushing to the bathroom. I followed her and was surprised to see her coughing up blood into the sink. For the first time in my life, I became really scared for my mom.

"Mom? Are you okay?" I asked.

As my mom turned to see me, she gasped and said, "Oh sweetie it's you... Umm, Mommy is just fine. I'm just feeling a little sick right now, that's all."

Even though Mom told me she was fine, deep down I knew something was wrong, but I just shrugged it off since I was only a kid at the time. As the years passed, Mom's health continued to get worse, until one day her chest started hurting her so much that she couldn't take it any longer. We took her to the emergency room where she was diagnosed with lung cancer and was told that she didn't have long to live. However, the doctors did say that with cryotherapy her health could improve.

Since our insurance couldn't afford the chemotherapy, we were forced to pay Mom's medical bills ourselves. Since I was seventeen at the time, I got a job at a fast-food joint. And Michael, being fifteen, worked as a local paperboy. Our Dad on the other hand had to work two jobs while also running the agency. Jim also tried to help by keeping the agency afloat by working as one of the agency's detectives.

When I turned twenty-three, I started looking into law school. I was thinking about becoming a lawyer so I could help pay mom's bills better. But college was too expensive for us, and we still needed to pay not only Mom's bills but so much more.

The stress eventually became too much for me, which led to me getting fired from my job for making too many mistakes at work. Michael also lost his job for the same reason, but he on the other hand assaulted his boss for firing him, which of course got him an invitation to a jail cell as he was arrested. When Michael called me using his one phone call, I paid his bail and went to get him out of jail.

Once I did get him out, I began lecturing him, "Michael please, you need to stop getting in trouble. I can't afford to pay another assault bail. I'm begging you, little brother, you're twenty-one years old now, start acting like it."

"I know, but my boss, he didn't appreciate anything I did! After working an eight-hour shift for the past five days, I make one goddamn mistake...and what happens? He fires me! I begged him to give me another chance, but he didn't want to hear what I had to say... And I just snapped because I knew that I needed that job to help pay for Mom's bills."

"Oh Michael, I'm so sorry. I know this entire situation has been stressful... for all of us. But that gives you no excuse for assaulting your boss!"

"Yeah, I know... Can you please just not tell Dad, since he's the one who is stressing the most from this?"

"Hmm, okay I won't. And yeah, you're right about that. Dad really has been the one stressing out the most..."

Shortly after, I got a call from Dad. He told us to go to the hospital as soon as possible. Once we arrived, we saw Dad talking with the doctor outside Mom's room. Observing Dad, I could tell he hadn't been sleeping well as I noticed dark circles under both of his eyes.

We asked Dad if something happened with Mom to which he replied, "No, nothing happened... But... Oh God, can you explain it to them, doctor?"

"Of course, Mr. Davis. Okay, your mother, she only has a few days left to live... The cancer has almost completely spread to her lungs. But as I was explaining to your father. The cancer hasn't spread to any other organ, meaning there could still be a chance to save your mother. By means of a lung transplant via surgery."

"But the surgery cost one million dollars... Which we don't have," Dad said, tearing up.

"What! But can't we sell something? What about my car?" Michael proposed.

"No, even if we did sell all our cars... It still wouldn't be enough for the surgery. I've even thought about selling the office of the agency... but that too won't cover it," Dad clarified.

It was at that point that we lost all hope of saving Mom. In the following days, we all tried to spend as much time as possible with Mom, talking with her, walking with her around the hospital, and even watching movies together. But one day Dad called me and Michael to go see him at the agency.

When we both arrived, we were first greeted by Jim who was at his desk. Jim told us that our dad was waiting for us in his office. Upon entering Dad's office, we found him seated at his desk with his head down.

After realizing that Dad was sleeping, I whispered to him to wake him up, "Hey Dad? Wake up Dad, it's us."

"Huh? Oh, hello boys. What brings you here?"

"Didn't you call us earlier? Don't you remember?"

"Oh, that's right... I'm sorry boys, it's just that I haven't been sleeping a lot lately. Okay, the reason I wanted you both to come at such short notice is that I believe I've found something that might make it possible for us to get the one million dollars and more."

"Wait, are you being serious? Oh my God, how?" Michael asked.

"Well, earlier today a group of men in black suits came to the agency and offered for me to do a job for them. They showed me a briefcase that was filled with stacks of cash. They said that it contained over ten million dollars!"

"Ten million dollars? Now that's a bit much... Are you sure that this isn't a scam? Because a scam is the last thing, we need during Mom's last days to live," I replied.

"I'm not sure, but... I need to at least try. This might be our only chance to save your mother!"

"But what if it isn't? What if something happens to you?"

"I'll be fine Connor. I promise you; I'll be back... Okay?"

"... Alright, you better."

Later that day, I was at the hospital with Mom. We were both watching her favorite show on television. Meanwhile, Michael was helping Dad prepare for the job. Apparently, the job Dad had to do was out of state in North Dakota which I found suspicious, but I trusted in Dad's judgment.

While watching Mom's show, I received a call from Michael which I proceeded to answer, "Hey Michael, are you done helping Dad?"

"Yeah, I have but... I'm deciding to go help Dad with the job. Dad is currently in no condition to be able to drive out of state on his own. So, I'll be the one driving him there."

"Wait what? So, I'm going to be the only one here?"

"Yeah, I'm sorry, but don't worry, we'll be back before you know it!"

"Hmm, okay, just promise me you won't do anything reckless... Okay?"

"Yeah, of course... I promise."

Hanging up, I turned to see mom smiling at me. I grabbed a chair nearby and sat next to her. She began patting my head and soon began to cry.

"I'm so proud of you and Michael... Especially your father. You've all worked so hard to pay my hospital bills. I hate how much of a burden I've become. I'm so sorry for putting this family through such an ordeal," Mom explained, rubbing her teary eyes.

"Mom, don't bring yourself down like that... None of this was your fault," I responded as I also began to cry.

Tears started flowing down her face as she muttered to me, "I know why all of you have been spending as much time with me as possible. I may not have much time left but just remember that we'll all see each other again one day. All I ask you is that you don't lose your faith and live life."

Nodding to my mom, I wiped her tears as she kept sobbing. I then gave her a big hug, not letting go of her. She hugged me back and we both began to cry together.

"I love you, Mom. Why did you have to get cancer? It's not fair!"

"I love you too sweetie, and I know it's not fair. But I just want you to remember this. God has a plan for all of us and everything that happens, whether it be good or bad, is for a reason."

Hearing Mom say those words did make me feel a bit better about the situation. It filled me with the hope that Dad and Michael could actually succeed. But that very hope soon became the dread that would haunt me for the rest of my life.

It was around midnight; Mom was sleeping in her hospital bed while I was preparing to fall asleep myself on the sleeper sofa. The television was still on but was on mute. When I went to turn it off, I suddenly received a call from an unknown number that I didn't recognize.

Answering the call, I proceeded to say the following, "Hello? Who is this?"

"Hello, is this Connor Davis?"

"Yes? Why are you calling me? How did you get this number?"

"Okay, my name is Joe Murphy, I'm the sheriff of Valley City. Alright now, I'm going to explain this to you very carefully. Your father, unfortunately, was in a car accident. We found his car crashed into a nearby tree... I'm so sorry."

"What? No, that's not true... He promised me that he was coming back!"

"Sir, I understand how you must be feeling, but that is the truth."

"What about my brother? Is he alive?"

"Brother? Umm, I'm afraid we only found your father's body. But again, I'm so very sorry for your loss."

Hanging up the phone, I dropped to my knees and began crying... It was at that moment that my entire world began to crumble. I felt like everything started to not matter anymore, even my own life. I began contemplating whether God really existed, but once I saw my mom sleeping, I remembered what she told me earlier. Swallowing my own grief, I sat down next to her. Not being able to sleep, I watched over her until morning.

By morning, I found mom dead, when I noticed the heart monitor flatline. The doctors came and tried reviving her, but she was already gone. A week later, Jim and I held their funeral at the local cemetery. I placed three white roses on each of their graves and stood there for hours, weeping.

After that, I didn't know what to do with my life. But since I was still unemployed, I decided to take over my dad's investigation agency. And the rest was history.

"… Oh my god, that was… I'm so sorry," the woman said.

"Yeah, well, they all died three years ago… so I've had some time to deal with the grief. But I don't think I would have been able to handle it the way I did if it weren't for Jim and my mom's last words…"

"… Anna, my name is Anna."

"What?"

"I just wanted you to know my name… in case we don't make it out alive."

"Heh, well, Anna is a pretty name… I'm glad I got to meet you. When we met, you saved me, and if it wasn't for you, I would have already been dead… Thank you, Anna."

"… Connor, I—" Anna said, but suddenly Mr. Dixon and his guards came into the room.

"Well, what do we have here?" said Mr. Dixon, approaching Connor and Anna.

Chapter 8
Confrontation

As Mr. Dixon approached Connor and Anna, his footsteps echoed in the room. Mr. Dixon first walked up to Anna and grabbed her by the face. Looking up and down at Anna, he licked his lips.

"Very nice, now you might make a pretty penny," Mr. Dixon said, smirking.

Once Mr. Dixon released his grasp on Anna's face, she reacted by head-butting him. As a result, Mr. Dixon responded by slapping her across the face. Witnessing this, Connor's eyes widened as he clenched his jaw.

"Don't you touch her!" Connor shouted.

When Mr. Dixon heard Connor shout at him, he turned around and said, "You, I know you... Haha, now this puts a smile on my face!"

"Dixon, please just let her go. Torture me instead if you want, just don't hurt her!"

"Wow, is it me or do you care a lot about this bitch?" Mr. Dixon said, raising one of his eyebrows.

"Please, I'm begging you. Don't do this."

"Hmm, you know what? I think I will torture you. Nicolas, get over here!"

"Umm, yes boss?"

"For the accomplishment in capturing the trespassers, I've decided to give you and the rest of the guards a reward... The woman, you, and the guards can do *anything* you want with her."

"Wait, what? No! Don't you dare—" Connor shouted, but had his head grabbed by Mr. Dixon.

"And you, I want you to *watch,* I want to make you suffer just like how you *people* made me suffer!"

Unable to move his head, Connor witnessed Nicolas order the rest of the guards to hold Anna down to the floor. Not knowing what Nicolas was planning to do, he tried to break free from his restraints, but it was to no avail. But the moment Nicolas started unbuckling his belt, his heart stopped.

"No! Please, Dixon, stop this!" Connor pleaded as he was tearing up.

"Stop this? Why would I do such a thing? Things are just getting *interesting*. Don't you agree?"

It was hopeless, there was nothing Connor could do. Feeling powerless, he tried praying again, hoping to have a miracle happen. However, he suddenly remembered the time Jim had trained him in some of his marine skills. Not knowing why, the memory of Jim showing him how to break free from restraints was more vivid to him than the rest of his training.

Acting immediately, Connor performed the technique taught to him. In a final effort, he clenched both hands and unraveled the rope once the restraints began to loosen. Finally having his hands free, he elbow-struck Mr. Dixon in the rib cage and proceeded to tackle Nicolas to the floor.

Having Nicolas pinned, Connor noticed a knife in Nicolas's pants and took hold of it. Using the knife, he stabbed Nicolas in the right leg, causing Nicolas to cry out in pain. When he stood back up, he found himself surrounded by the rest of the guards.

Standing his ground, Connor raised his clenched fists and got into a fighting stance. With his eyes glancing at each guard, he saw them all preparing themselves as they reached for their weapons. It was only when he saw one of the guards cock their pistol that he charged and tackle the guard. Taking hold of the guard's pistol he proceeded to knock out the guard with a jab to the head.

After having knocked out one of the guards, Connor then began receiving gunfire from the other guards. While the rest of the guards shot at him, he quickly slid behind one of the pillars and evaded the gunfire. When the gunfire eventually subsided, he seized the opening and used the guard's pistol and shot at the room's lights, plunging the room into darkness.

With the guards blinded by the darkness of the room, Connor swiftly took out the rest of the guards, one by one. Having taken out all the guards, he stood holding the hair of one of the guards, catching his breath. Thinking it was over, he began to settle down until he heard Anna scream. He turned around and saw Mr. Dixon holding Anna at gunpoint.

"Alright, if you want this bitch to live, I suggest you give up now," Mr. Dixon said, holding Anna hostage.

Seeing Anna used as a human shield, Connor's eyes widened. Keeping his eyes on Mr. Dixon, he clenched both his fists. As if he was about to explode, he was overtaken by adrenaline.

"You let her go… Or I'm gonna tear you apart," Connor said as his breathing intensified.

"Oh really? Well, come on then!"

Clenching his fists tighter, Connor unleashed a roaring scream as he charged at Mr. Dixon. Meanwhile, Mr. Dixon chuckled at the sight and threw Anna to the side. Likewise, Mr. Dixon also let out a roaring scream at Connor and charged at him as well. With both charging at the other, it seemed like they were going to crash. However, Connor slid underneath Mr. Dixon, climbed behind him, and began arm-choking him.

As a result, Mr. Dixon began thrashing around the room, trying to get Connor to let go. But it was to no avail as Connor used all his strength to lock his arms around Mr. Dixon's neck. Thinking he had Mr. Dixon beaten, Connor smirked, continuing to choke Mr. Dixon. However, Connor's smirk soon subsided once Mr. Dixon began charging toward the door.

Just when Mr. Dixon was about to crash into the door, he turned around, making Connor take the impact. After smashing through the door, Connor felt as if his body had been crushed. Struggling to get up, he looked up and saw Mr. Dixon, who was also striving to stand up.

Once they were both back on their feet, Mr. Dixon began frantically throwing punches at Connor. Although Connor was able to dodge a few punches, he was staggered and had difficulty standing due to the impact of the door. Thus, Mr. Dixon managed to strike Connor several times and was even able to grab ahold of his head and smash it against the wall.

"This is revenge for when you people killed my father!" Mr. Dixon shouted.

"Wait, what? Who killed your father?" Connor asked, rubbing blood off his nose.

"Still denying that you're one of them. Well, deny it all you want, you're not leaving this casino alive!"

Having multiple bruises, it seemed hopeless for Connor. However, on the floor, in the corner of his eye, he noticed Anna was aiming a pistol at Mr. Dixon. Turning around to see what she was aiming at, he witnessed Mr. Dixon getting shot in the arm.

Mr. Dixon cried out in pain, and when Anna was about to shoot Mr. Dixon again, he grabbed Anna by the neck. As Mr. Dixon attempted to strangle Anna, Connor stepped in by gut-punching Mr. Dixon in the stomach. This caused Mr. Dixon to let go of Anna.

Connor followed up with another punch, striking Mr. Dixon's jaw. He continued punching Mr. Dixon and even managed to knock out a tooth from Mr. Dixon. However, just as Connor was about to deliver a left hook, Mr. Dixon grabbed his arm and hurled him into a door nearby.

Having been thrown into yet another door, Connor found himself in another room. The room appeared to be a conference room and had a red carpet for its floor. When he was about to stand back up, Mr. Dixon stomped his foot onto his chest.

"You thought... that you could just come to *my casino* and take me down just like that? It's funny, you tried taking the legal route first by prosecuting me in court, and that failed! Now, you've trespassed onto my property and have assaulted countless of my guards... and look where that got you."

"Well, at least tell me why… Why would you choose to do something so awful, so horrible that you'd sell other human beings."

"What? Is that why you're here? Oh, I see… You really aren't one of them. Well, even if you aren't, it doesn't matter. I'm still going to kill you," Mr. Dixon said, getting on top of Connor and began choking him.

As Connor struggled to break free, his strength began to dwindle. At that moment, he began to doubt whether he should continue fighting. He even began imagining himself reunited with his family. But when he thought of Jim and Anna, he couldn't forget them. *I have to keep fighting… for them.* And thus, he looked for a way to break free and noticed the gunshot wound on Mr. Dixon's arm.

Clenching his fist, Connor delivered a punch to the gunshot wound, causing Mr. Dixon to scream. As a result, Mr. Dixon released his grip on Connor's throat, which allowed Connor to kick Mr. Dixon away. As Mr. Dixon cried out on the floor, he stomped on Mr. Dixon's gunshot wound, inflicting even more pain on Mr. Dixon.

After that, it was Connor who got on top of Mr. Dixon and began punching Mr. Dixon in the face. However, Connor wouldn't stop and just continued to punch Mr. Dixon over and over again. It was almost like he entered a state of pure rage that blinded him with hatred.

Eventually, Mr. Dixon's face swelled up, and blood splattered on the carpet nearby due to the continuous punching. With each punch Connor threw at Mr. Dixon's face, the bloodier Mr. Dixon's face came to be. To finish Mr. Dixon off, Connor yanked on Mr. Dixon's suit and raised his arm so he could deliver the finishing punch. But just when he was about to finish Mr. Dixon off, he halted. He recalled what Jim had told him before when he was in the same situation.

"No, I can't…" Connor muttered.

"Haha, what's the matter? You can't bring yourself to kill me? Come on, kill me!"

"No! No matter how much I want to kill you… I won't let you destroy who I am!"

"Then what are you going to do? Try and prosecute me back in court again? Face it! There is nothing you can do to stop me!"

"… No, but you *will* face justice. It may not be in this world but once you die… God will make you pay for *everything* you've done. Since wrath belongs to God and God alone."

Walking away from Mr. Dixon Connor thought it was finally over, but when he walked into the hallway, suddenly, he was surrounded by more guards. Observing the guards surrounding him, he noticed Anna was also held captive, with one of the guards aiming a pistol at her head.

"I'm sorry but I think you have forgotten that you're still in *my* casino. You may have won the fight, but you can't win the war, no matter how determined you are," Mr. Dixon said, as one of the guards helped him stand back up.

Following this, Connor and Anna were forced to stand against the curtain wall that overlooked the city. While they stood there in anticipation, Mr. Dixon, struggling to stand up, was handed a pistol from one of the guards. With the pistol in hand, Mr. Dixon slowly approached Connor and pressed it against Connor's forehead.

"You wanna know something? You are the first person in a long time that has ever bested me in a fight... And for that, you have my respect."

"I don't want your respect."

"Hmm, I had a feeling you'd say that... Oh well, I suppose it's time we finally end this feud of ours for good," Mr. Dixon said in the process of pulling the trigger of the pistol.

However, just as Mr. Dixon was about to pull the trigger, Connor noticed a red dot on Mr. Dixon's forehead. In the blink of an eye, Mr. Dixon was sniped right in front of Connor and Anna, shattering the curtain wall behind them. Before the guards could even react themselves, they were all shot and killed, one after another.

Speechless, Connor and Anna froze while they witnessed everyone getting killed off. Not knowing what to do, Connor began to contemplate the chaos. *What is happening? Who is the one killing everyone?* Anna on the other hand came back to her senses and saw an opportunity for them to escape.

Thus, Anna grabbed hold of Connor's arm and shouted, "Connor, now is our chance! Let's go!"

Coming back to his senses as well, Connor nodded at Anna. As the two proceeded to run, they eventually came across a stairwell. Just before they went down the stairs, Anna's eyes widened and looked back.

When Connor saw Anna glancing back, he asked her, "Anna, what's wrong?"

"Madison's document... It's still in the room where we were held captive. If I lose that document, I lose my only hope of finding Madison. I'm sorry Connor, but I need to go and find that document!" Anna said as she ran back.

"What? Anna, wait!" Connor said, going after Anna.

Running through the hallways, they'd stumble upon the corpses of the guards from before, with nearly all of them murdered. Although some were still alive, seeing their injuries were so severe, Connor knew there was little chance of them surviving. *Who was this sniper? And why did they only spare me and Anna?* Even though the whole situation puzzled him, he had to put his thoughts aside once they had arrived at the room.

Now in the room, Anna began searching for the document. Connor tried to help, but because he had shot at the room's lights earlier, they were unable to find anything in the dark. Nonetheless, as he searched, Connor noticed bloody shoe prints that stained the floor.

Following the shoe prints, he saw that they were all around him. While he pondered who could have left them, he suddenly heard footsteps behind him. Turning around to see who was approaching, he saw Nicolas running toward him with the same knife he had stabbed Nicolas's leg with earlier.

Slashing the knife at Connor, Nicolas managed to cut Connor's left arm. This created an opportunity for Nicolas to go in for the kill. However, Nicolas was shot by Anna in the back. Having shot Nicolas, Nicolas tried to crawl away, leaving a trail of blood. With a blank expression, Anna aimed her pistol at Nicolas, cornering him against the wall. Right when Anna was about to pull the trigger, Nicolas took out Madison's document and held it over the flame of a lighter.

"This is what you're looking for right? Well, you better not shoot, or else I'll burn this precious document of yours," Nicolas uttered.

With a glare directed at Nicolas, Anna lowered her pistol reluctantly. Nicolas chuckled at Anna's obedience as he tried standing back up but fell back down due to his gunshot wound.

Realizing this, Connor walked up to Nicolas and said, "Nicolas, you need to stop this… You're bleeding out and you can hardly move. There's nothing you're going to gain from this. Please, just give us the document."

"You're wrong, if I kill you, I'll be promoted. I will be made Mr. Dixon's right-hand man!"

"Well, I hate to break it to you, but Dixon is dead! So are the rest of the guards!" Anna shouted.

"What? Heh, now that's some bullshit right there."

"It's true! We're not sure, but there was this sniper that came out of nowhere… and started killing everyone," Connor explained.

"… Except you two. Hmm, now why is that?"

"I don't know… but that doesn't matter right now. What does matter is what choice you are going to make. Are you going to keep trying to kill us? Or are you going to stop this nonsense?"

As Nicolas looked down, Connor gulped, not knowing what Nicolas was going to do. But his eyebrows lifted when he saw that Nicolas had turned off his lighter and handed the document to Anna. Seeing this, Connor smiled, knowing Nicolas was now on the path to righteousness. But once Anna received her document, she punched Nicolas in the face, knocking him out.

"Was that really necessary?" Connor asked.

"After everything he did… Yes, it was."

Once they had gone down the stairwell, the two finally exited the building. Closing his eyes, Connor took a deep breath, knowing they'd survived. However, it was at that moment he realized that this could be the last time he'd see Anna.

Turning his head to look at Anna, Connor says, "So, you going to go to that address and try to find your sister?'

"Yeah, I finally have something that could actually help me find her," Anna said, clenching onto Madison's document.

"I see… Something terrible is happening in this city and I need to find out what that is."

"Well, I wish you the best of luck… and may God bless you. But if you don't mind, here's my number. It would be a good idea if we stayed in touch. So, we could maybe help each other in the future?" Anna said, handing Connor a piece of paper with her number.

"Oh, that would be a good idea. Heh, you know what? I'll also give you mine since we're exchanging numbers… Alright then, I guess this is goodbye," Connor said as he also handed Anna his phone number.

"Yeah, I guess… For now, at least," Anna said, walking away.

Chapter 9
Secrets Unfold

Now on his own, Connor traversed downtown and managed to reach the hotel building he and Jim were staying at. Remembering what Chief Willie said to him about sending officers to kill Jim made his heart race. As he went up the stairwell, he dreaded what he'd find. Finally arriving on their floor, he gasped when he saw blood staining the doorknob.

With his eyes widened, Connor slowly reached out his hand and grabbed the doorknob. After opening the door, the first thing he saw was a dead police officer who had his head shot. When he entered the hallway, his heart stopped when he witnessed multiple dead bodies of more police officers scattered throughout the hallway.

Walking past the corpses of battered officers, Connor noticed how the officers were all massacred. *Who could have done this? Could Jim have been responsible? No, that's ridiculous, he wouldn't be capable of doing any of this.* Shaking his head, he gulped when he finally approached their room door. Once he got there, he saw another officer lying dead at the entrance. Inspecting the officer, he noticed that the officer was shot in the head and had a bloody bruise on the left side of his head.

Entering their hotel room, Connor saw how the room was trashed. He even caught a glimpse of yet another officer dead with their faces beaten to the point of being unrecognizable. There was no sight of Jim or anyone alive when he looked around. He figured that Jim most likely escaped and made it out alive. Putting his hand on his chin, he pondered on who could've been responsible for killing all the officers.

Inspecting the room, he searched for anything that could be of some use to him. Searching under his bed, he found his suitcase and when he opened it, he found new clothes and his wallet. He also was able to find his tools, such as his magnifying glass, his handheld black light, and his binoculars.

As Connor put the three tools in his satchel, he also put on the new clothes he found in his suitcase. Getting dressed, he noticed his trench coat hanging on the closet hanger. Putting on his trench coat, he was now ready to continue his search for answers. He figured if he wanted to find out what was happening, city hall would be the first place he should investigate.

When reaching city hall, Connor had second thoughts about breaking into it. *To think, I was so supportive in following the law… and now I'm breaking into city hall of all places.* Putting aside his unsettling thoughts, he reminded himself that he had a mission to uncover the truth.

Approaching city hall, he looked around the building for a way to get inside. Having no luck in finding anything, he had to think outside the box. Looking around, he noticed a pickup truck parked nearby, which sparked an idea. Searching the pickup truck's cargo bed, he found a toolbox and a crowbar.

Grabbing the crowbar his thoughts turned to how to use it, without making too much noise. Taking note of the many windows city hall had, he came up with a risky idea. Though he was unable to reach one of the windows, he took a second look at the pickup truck, which gave him another idea.

By climbing onto the pickup truck, he finally managed to reach one of the windows. Using the crowbar, he was able to pry open the window and slide it up. Looking inside, he found the architecture rather enchanting. Yet despite the grandness of the building, he shook his head and jumped down.

Once Connor landed on the floor, he then put on his hood as he then began inspecting the area. Searching for any clues, he checked one of the offices. However, just before he could search for anything, he heard footsteps nearby. Taking cover behind a desk, he lingered until they passed.

"Hey, I think I heard something," a security guard said, roaming the halls.

"It's probably just the wind," another security guard said, taking out a cigarette.

"Maybe… Huh? What the hell are you doing dipshit? You can't smoke in here, it's city hall!"

"Oh, come on! A quick smoke won't hurt anyone. Besides, this job is boring enough as it is," the security guard said, lighting his cigarette.

As the two security guards continued to walk down the hallway, the guards soon came across a dark wooden door. The door seemed more prominent than the other doors as it was the only door that had a different color. This got Connor scratching his head but would continue to focus on what the two guards were saying.

Following their arrival at the door, the security guard that was smoking gazed at it and said, "To think that this used to once be Mayor Johnson's office… May his soul rest in peace."

"Amen… I never liked him as mayor though," the other security guard remarked.

"Heh, yeah raising the city's taxes was ridiculous. Like, what was he thinking? And have you read the newspaper? It says that the city council is going to do exactly that! I mean come on; they should at least increase the minimum wage… Well anyways, I guess it's time we head back down and monitor the surveillance," the security guard said, exhaling smoke from the cigarette.

"Yeah, we should… Also, can you *please* stop smoking indoors, it's rude," the other security guard said as they both walked down the stairway.

After the security guards left, Connor stood up and approached the mayor's office door. Knowing that the office belonged to the mayor, Connor realized it was the best place where he could find some answers. Attempting to open the office door, his eyebrows lowered, finding it to be locked.

To open the door, he searched for something he could use. Rummaging through the other offices' desks, he found a box of paper clips, which gave him an idea. By bending two paper clips precisely, he contrived a makeshift lock pick from the paper clips.

Using the makeshift lock pick, Connor was able to unlock the mayor's office. Entering the office, he found it to be vacant, with no one in sight. Beginning to search the office for any clue, he came across a letter on the mayor's desk. He noticed that it was hidden beneath a desk lamp. Proceeding to lift the lamp, he took hold of the letter. The letter talked about the state of Minnesota granting Mayor Johnson approval to raise the city's taxes. Realizing the letter gave him useless information, he tossed it aside. But after he threw it, he noticed some scribbles on the back of the letter.

Flipping the letter, Connor saw sketches of a vase, rug, desk, and picture frame. Holding onto his chin he pondered on what the drawings meant. Looking around, he strangely enough found all those items in the mayor's office. Contemplating what it all meant, he decided to take a guess and inspect each item in its order.

Checking each item, to his surprise, he found that they all had a number written on them. The vase had the number eight written beneath it, the rug also had the number three written under it, and the desk had the number one written on one of the desk legs. However, when it came to the picture frame, what he found behind it left him with a gaping jaw.

Behind the picture frame, he discovered a hidden safe equipped with a keypad lock. Looking back at all the numbers he found on each item, excluding the picture frame, he entered the numbers into the keypad lock. After entering all the numbers, the safe opened when he heard it click.

Once the safe opened, Connor gulped, not knowing what he would find inside. Taking a glance inside the safe, what he found sent chills down his spine. Inside the safe was the same mask worn by the masked people, who appeared in the surveillance footage back in Mr. Dixon's casino. Besides the mask, he also found the same black cloak worn by the masked people.

With this in mind, Connor came to an unsettling conclusion. Following this, he took the mask and cloak with him and packed them in his satchel. Leaving city hall, the same way he came in, he left with several thoughts racing through his mind. Among the many thoughts he had, he pondered who else was involved.

He still lacked enough information to make sense of what was going on. Thinking of where else he could investigate next, he thought of Briana's apartment and how Chief Willie was so insistent that The Mortem was the one to blame for her murder. Considering all the information he'd now learned; he wondered what other lies Chief Willie might have told him.

Following that, Connor arrived by taxi at Brianna's apartment building with the little cash he had in his wallet. Climbing up the stairs, he became agitated about what he might find. He also recalled the horrors he had witnessed before.

Arriving on Briana's apartment floor, he noticed police tape was covering her door. Turning the knob on her door, he discovered it was locked. This led him to try and think of ways to break in. By observing how old the building was, he settled on a simpler method to break in.

So, by kicking the door down, Connor managed to gain entry. Upon entering Briana's apartment, his eyebrows lifted when he saw cleaning supplies scattered everywhere. While most of the evidence of Briana's murder was gone, he knew something had to remain to explain what was happening.

Searching the apartment, he first inspected where Briana was found dead. However, most of the bloodstains and evidence were removed by bleach, seeing as there was an unopened bleach bottle nearby. But what caught his eye would be a couple of bloody trash bags in the corner of the living room.

Approaching the trash bags, Connor gasped once he smelled the stench that stemmed from the bags. The stench was unlike anything he'd ever smelled before. It almost smelt like something that had been rotting away for days.

Before searching the trash bags, Connor looked around and found a box of disposable plastic gloves. Putting on a pair of gloves, he proceeded to open one of the bloody trash bags. But the moment he opened the bags, he nearly vomited when he witnessed the most horrendous thing he had ever seen.

Upon looking back into the trash bag, Connor saw a skinless human corpse that was dismembered. The sight was so repulsive it made him nauseated to the point where he puked on the floor. In the middle of trying to make sense of what he had just seen, he heard sudden footsteps approaching.

Staying behind a couch, Connor tried his best to remain silent. As he struggled to control his breathing, he had to listen to every step taken by whoever was entering the apartment. When he glanced behind himself, he saw two men wearing biohazard suits. He figured the two men were the ones cleaning the apartment.

Dismissing the two men, Connor began to contemplate everything. However, he suddenly heard a loud clattering that sounded almost like high heels closing in. Glimpsing to see who would be entering, his jaw dropped when he saw Briana Harper.

As soon as Connor saw Briana, he felt like he was going insane. In a formal pantsuit, Briana appeared to be alive and well despite remembering that he had just inspected her corpse a couple of days ago. Despite being more confused than ever, he knew he now needed to figure out what was happening.

"Ugh, look at this place. You two better get this place cleaned up by tomorrow," Briana said to the two men wearing biohazard suits.

"Of course, ma'am. We'll have it done before you know it," answered one of the men wearing the biohazard suit.

"Good because you don't want to upset *The Grand-Master*. Alright, I shall be leaving now, but when I return, I expect this place to be spotless," Briana said, walking out of the apartment.

Once Briana left, Connor knew he needed to follow her. Glancing around, he noticed a window nearby. From the window, he saw a fire escape leading to the ground. Exiting through the window, he made his way down the fire escape.

On the ground, he saw Briana walking down the sidewalk but lost sight of her as Briana passed another building. Rushing to catch up with Briana, he ran to the sidewalk hoping to find her, but his eyes widened when she was nowhere to be found. However, instead of finding Briana, he found Nancy, of all people walking up to a limousine. But what puzzled him the most was that Nancy was wearing the exact same clothes Briana was just wearing.

While Connor stood there attempting to understand what he saw, Nancy entered the limousine and drove off. Standing against the wall, he began to collect himself, trying to piece together everything. Knowing he was getting closer to uncovering the truth, he thought of where to investigate next. Going through his options in his head, he noticed a homeless man sleeping in his makeshift camp in an alleyway. As soon as he saw this, he immediately thought of the one place that could hold the last piece of this unsettling puzzle.

Upon arriving at the motel where The Mortem was torturing the mayor, Connor knew this was the place that held the answer to everything. However, he noticed something seemed off as there was nobody. It was like the motel was abandoned, as he was the only person in the area.

Wondering why this was the case, Connor shrugged it off as he returned his attention to The Mortem's motel room. While walking through the parking lot, his mind wandered back to see two police officers die in front of him by The Mortem. The image of those officers killed in cold blood made him think twice about entering the motel room again. However, he decided to swallow his worries and prepared himself for the worst.

Coming across The Mortem's motel room door, Connor began trembling, gazing at it. After finding the doorknob locked, he looked around and found a cinder block close by. Having smashed the doorknob, he proceeded to enter the room.

The entire room seemed intact from the last time he was there. So, he searched the room, but what he found was just what he had already uncovered. Trying to think of a way to find something he wasn't seeing; he remembered the handheld black light he had in his satchel.

Taking out his black light, he shined the light all over the room. Eventually, he noticed something glowing on top of a cabinet. Inspecting the cabinet, he found what appeared to be a stain that glowed under his flashlight. However, what he found strange was that the stain was invisible without the black light. Whatever it was, he assumed it had spilled on the cabinet, wondering what was inside the drawers. Opening each drawer, he came across a worn-down journal.

"Now what do we have here?" Connor remarked.

Opening the journal, his jaw dropped when he saw all the pages were blank. Trying to figure out why the journal was blank; he was stuck until an idea occurred to him. Using his black light, he shined it over the pages of the journal, which revealed numerous daily logs and other writings.

"This journal… It's written with some kind of invisible ink. Hmm, now things just keep getting interesting," Connor said, skimming through the journal.

January 12, 1999: I've tracked down the low life that is the governor of Oklahoma to an estate in Tulsa. That bastard thinks he can hide from me, but there is no hiding. I will find him and beat the coward to death until he stops moving. After that, I'm going to set that estate on fire to send a message to these cunts that I'm coming for them all.

"This guy really is messed up… So, I guess it's true… He really was going on a killing spree, murdering government officials. This journal log is kind of early. Let's see what the last thing this guy wrote," Connor said, skipping to the end of the journal.

August 21, 2002: After successfully abducting the mayor of Minneapolis, I've been torturing the bastard to get as much information as possible before he dies from blood loss. So far, he's told me the location of where he and his friends all meet up to do their disgusting rituals. Apparently, to gain entry, you must say the password *Ave bestia* to the guard at the front of the door. Slowly but surely, I'm getting closer to finding the one who's been pulling the strings to this whole shit show.

"Ave bestia? That kind of sounds like Latin… Alright, I think I have everything I need to know," Connor said, taking the blood-stained journal with him.

When Connor was about to leave, he suddenly heard men conversing from the other side of the door. Thinking fast, he quickly hid under the motel bed. To avoid making a sound, he tried to control his breathing.

Hearing the room door open, Connor heard one of the men speak, "Huh? That's strange, the doorknob has been smashed… Someone was here."

To remain silent, Connor covered his mouth with his hand. When the men entered the motel room, he heard the creaking of the floor. Glancing at the feet of the men, something of them seemed familiar. Taking a closer look from under the bed, he got a glimpse of one of the men and realized that these were police officers.

But when Connor glanced at the other two officers, he felt his heart stop once he saw Chief Willie standing with them. Just by seeing Chief Willie, chills ran down his spine as he remembered how Chief Willie left him to die back at the casino. Taking his hand out of his mouth, he clenched his fists tightly, recalling everything Chief Willie had said and done.

Despite his rage, Connor took a deep breath and unclenched his fists. Thinking of how he could escape the room, an idea came to his mind. Now waiting for the right moment to act, he lingered under the bed. It was only until Chief Willie checked the bathroom that he acted. Once he got out from under the bed, he grabbed hold of a nearby lamp and hurled it at the two officers. After that, he ran out of the room, leaving with The Mortem's journal.

Fleeing the motel, Connor ran as fast as he could and headed into the same alleyway that he had chased The Mortem from before. However, just as he was about to enter the alleyway, in the blink of an eye, a bullet hit his shoulder. As a result, he fell to the ground, crying out in pain. With his eyes widened, he slowly shifted his gaze onto his shoulder, seeing his gunshot wound. Struggling to stand back up, he turned to see Chief Willie aiming his pistol at him.

Afraid to move, Connor thought about how he could get out of Chief Willie's line of sight. Looking to his right, he got an idea as he saw a dumpster. As he built up courage, he stood up and leaped behind the dumpster, escaping Chief Willie's view.

As a result, Chief Willie snapped and started shooting repeatedly at the dumpster. Eventually, Chief Willie ran out of bullets and had to reload his pistol. As a result, Connor had enough time to move forward while hugging the wall. In the alleyways, Connor began searching for a place to hide. Emerging from the alley, he came across a street with a construction site nearby. Although he thought about hiding there, there wouldn't be many hiding spots, but a parking garage building next to the construction site seemed the more promising place for him to hide.

On the second floor of the building, Connor hid behind one of the many parked cars. He considered himself lucky to have found this building since it provided plenty of hiding spots for him. Despite all this, he was still suffering from pain in his shoulder caused by being shot.

Taking his shirt off, Connor began to inspect his gunshot wound. Seeing as the bullet only went through his shoulder, he presumed it was nothing more than a flesh wound. Nonetheless, he was still bleeding and applied pressure onto his gunshot wound with one hand. Using his other hand, he checked his satchel for anything he could use. His eyebrows lifted when he found the blue handkerchief Jim had given him to clean up his bloody hands.

Using the handkerchief, he wrapped his shoulder, making a makeshift bandage. After he finished patching himself up, he suddenly heard footsteps approaching. Putting his shirt back on, he glanced back and saw Chief Willie and his two officers.

"If you're in here, there's nowhere you can run. I've already called for a dozen more officers to arrive and soon this entire area will be swarmed with officers. But there's no need for violence, we can end this peacefully… If you just give up," Chief Willie said, pulling out his pistol.

Nodding to the two other officers, Chief Willie and the two officers began searching the area. Meanwhile, Connor did his best to stay quiet and tried to think of what he could do to escape. Thus, he came up with a plan on how to take out the two officers first.

Lurking within the parked cars, Connor decided to take out one officer at a time. So, he crept towards one of the officers, and while standing behind a car, he thought of a way to distract him. Taking out his wallet, he took out a penny and threw it against another car, attracting the officer's attention.

When the officer went to check what made the noise, Connor ran and tackled the officer. Having the officer pinned to the floor, he punched the officer repeatedly. With each punch he threw at the officer's face, he made more noise in beating the officer up. Knowing he needed to finish off the officer as quickly as possible, he clenched his fists and struck the officer's face so hard that he knocked out the officer instantly.

After rendering the officer unconscious, in an instant, Connor stood up and ran to the nearest parked car for cover. With his back to a car, he hid as he watched Chief Willie and the other officer arrive. Upon their arrival, Chief Willie and the other officer found the unconscious officer lying on the floor. Chief Willie crouched down and checked the unconscious officer's pulse.

"Is he alive? Holy shit, what if we're dealing with The Mortem?" the other officer said, breathing heavily.

"He's alive, he's only been knocked out… And based on the many reports I've read, if this was The Mortem, we would already be dead by now," Chief Willie clarified.

"I see… Then who are we dealing with here?"

"I got a few ideas but so far, I'm not sure… But whoever did this is close by, so we'll split up, and if you find something you let me know. Remember we don't want to upset The Grand-Master."

With Chief Willie and the other officer splitting up, Connor knew this worked to his advantage. Devising a plan, he decided to take out the other officer and thought about using the same tactic he had used on the first officer. Sneaking up to the other officer, he tried taking out another penny from his wallet, but the penny slipped out of his hand and fell on the floor. The other officer got alerted as the officer heard the penny falling. Noticing a corner mirror nearby, the officer saw Connor crouched behind a parked car.

"Chief, I found something! Hurry before—" the other officer blurted out but got tackled by Connor.

After pinning the other officer, Connor attempted to knock the officer out as he had done with the first officer. But his eyes widened once the other officer struck him back. Being punched in the face by the other officer, he realized that this officer was more skilled than the other.

However, the officer flinched when he saw Chief Willie running toward him. As a result, Connor managed to knock the pistol out of the officer's hands. Having disarmed the officer, Connor punched the officer in the stomach, resulting in the officer collapsing on the floor. Grabbing hold of the officer's head, Connor smashed the officer's head against a car, knocking the officer unconscious.

Once Connor had knocked out the last officer, he gasped for air, regaining his composure. Standing back up, he turned to look and saw Chief Willie aiming a pistol at him. Neither of them uttered a word and just stared down at the other.

The silence between the two only broke when Chief Willie proceeded to say, "Connor... Now, this truly is a shocking sight. I would ask how you managed to escape from Mr. Dixon's casino but that's no longer important now. But what I am going to say to you, I am going to say once and *only* once... You are going to raise your hands and I'm going to handcuff you. If you don't cooperate, I will shoot—" Chief Willie said but in an instant's notice Connor ducked behind a parked car, and when Connor did so, Chief Willie opened fire.

Following would be a barrage of bullets coming from Chief Willie. Managing to hide behind a concrete pillar, Connor waited for the rest of the gunfire coming from Chief Willie. As he remained behind the pillar, he noticed a van that seemed to be entering the building. Realizing it was his chance to escape, he took a leap of faith and jumped from the second floor of the parking garage building. Luckily, he managed to land on top of the van, but it came at the cost of his left arm broken by the impact.

Due to Connor landing on top of the van, the driver stopped, allowing Connor to get off. The driver exited the van and was a middle-aged man who scratched his head about what happened. The middle-aged man looked around and saw Connor running toward the construction site.

"Hey! Are you crazy? God damn psycho—" the middle-aged man said, but got shot by Chief Willie, who finally made it down from the second floor.

Meanwhile, Connor arrived at the construction site and looked for somewhere to hide. He was thinking of hiding behind the bulldozer, but after thinking it over, he decided it may not be the best idea. Eventually, he came across the unfinished building they were constructing and decided to hide behind one of its walls.

While he hid, he checked his arm and confirmed it was broken. However, since the pain wasn't as severe, he concluded it was a minor fracture. After a few minutes, he stayed there where he contemplated his next move.

"Connor! Do you think you can hide from me? Having jumped off a building, you *must* have broken something," Chief Willie said, inspecting the area of the construction site.

In response to Chief Willie's mockery, Connor shouted, "Oh yeah? Well, I never thought that you were a dirty cop all along. Tell me, what's it like being the very thing you were supposed to fight against? After everything, we've been through... I thought you were my friend for God's sake! I trusted you!"

"It was never personal Connor... I did what I had to do! It's my job!"

"Right, and what exactly is your job? You, the mayor, Nancy, the entire police force... Who else is involved in your crazy cult that I don't know about yet?"

When Chief Willie heard Connor's question, Chief Willie became speechless. Connor noticed this and reacted by making a run for it. But Chief Willie came back to his senses as he heard Connor's footsteps. Once Chief Willie spotted Connor, he started firing, but lost sight of him when Connor hid behind a concrete mixer truck.

Having fired numerous bullets, Chief Willie ran out of ammunition again and had to reload his pistol. But as he was about to reload his pistol, Connor tackled him. To grab the pistol and magazine, the two wrestled each other on the ground.

It was ultimately futile as Chief Willie overthrew Connor, who delivered a punch to Connor's gunshot wound. With one last attempt to knock out Chief Willie, Connor tried to grab ahold of Chief Willie's jacket but felt an unbearable pain from his broken arm. After putting up with the pain of his broken arm and a gunshot wound, he looked up only to see Chief Willie aiming at him with the loaded pistol.

"It's over Connor... You can't run this time."

"You don't have to do this chief... It's not too late. Is this really what you want to be? A murderer? What would your mother think of you? You think she'd be proud of who you've become?"

Listening to Connor's words, Chief Willie looked at his pistol in silence. He then looked around and saw the middle-aged man he had just killed moments ago. Upon seeing this, he burst into tears and fell to his knees.

Seeing Chief Willie break down before him, Connor stood up and walked over to him, saying, "Hey, it's okay there's still a chance for you to redeem yourself... For starters, you could tell me the truth about everything."

"I can't... I swore an oath and if I break it, they will kill my mother."

"What? What do you mean by oath? Who's they? And why are they going to kill your mother?"

"All I can tell you is that they are everywhere. There's no place on earth where you're safe from their control... But you still have a chance to escape. Quickly, you need to run before the rest of my officers arrive."

"Well, let's go together. You don't have to continue doing their dirty work anymore. Come on, fight for what's right."

"I'm sorry, but it's too late for me... I've done too much... I just want it to all end," Chief Willie said, glancing at his pistol on the ground.

Slowly extending his arm, Chief Willie took hold of his pistol. Having his pistol clutched in his hand, he held it at the side of his head. But before pulling the trigger, he took one last glance at Connor.

"Take care of yourself Connor... and I'm sorry," Chief Willie said, smiling as he pulled the trigger on his pistol.

Chapter 10
Revelations

When Connor saw Chief Willie take his own life, he became speechless as it took a while to process what had just happened. Gazing upon Chief Willie's lifeless body, he cried out. As he continued crying out, he fell to his knees, beginning to feel light-headed until he eventually passed out on the ground.

Waking up, Connor felt a stinging sensation on one of his shoulders. Opening his eyes, he saw Jim pouring hydrogen peroxide on the gunshot wound that he had in his shoulder. Looking around, he noticed they were inside a van.

Turning to look at Jim, Connor asked, "Jim, where are we?"

In response to Connor waking up, Jim immediately reached out and hugged him. Connor embraced Jim back and they both began to cry while hugging each other. After Connor and Jim hugged each other, Connor thought about what he should say.

In a tearful gaze, Connor looked at Jim and said, "I'm so sorry for what I said at the casino… I didn't know what I was saying."

"No, I'm sorry. I shouldn't have abandoned you… I left you after I promised that I wouldn't disappear on you."

After that, the two smiled at one another, and as they hugged again, they burst into laughter. However, Connor's smile soon subsided as he fell silent. As his eyes widened, he began to recall everything that had happened.

"Jim, there's something I need to tell you… it's something I know this is all going to sound crazy, but I found out at the casino when I was with… Chief Willie. There's this secret society of masked people who secretly control the city. And the scariest part is that these people are all the city officials and pretty much anyone who has some kind of political power. Which includes Nancy and… Chief Willie."

"Really? I'm sure it must have been hard for you to learn… the truth," Jim said, glancing at the driver's seat of the van.

Raising one eyebrow, Connor wondered why Jim so easily believed him. Despite suspecting Jim of hiding something, he continued to explain all that had happened to him. And after hearing everything, Jim's expression soon shifted to one of despair.

With tearful eyes, Jim looked at Connor and said, "And this all happened after I left?"

"Yes... But there's still one thing that I can't figure out. The sniper that saved Anna and me. If it wasn't for that sniper, we would have already been dead... I don't know why but thinking about that sniper reminds me of when I chased after The Mortem in the alleyway. Why didn't he kill me when he had the chance? I was knocked unconscious, and he had the opportunity to shoot me. You think there might be a connection?"

"Maybe... But what's important is that you're alive."

"Yeah, let's thank God and the holy spirit for that... Anyway, back to my first question. Where are we? Like, I can see that we're inside a van."

"Ah, well that's a bit difficult to answer... Let's say that an old friend is helping us. It took us a while, but we were able to find you on the ground unconscious at that construction site. And luckily, I was able to take out the bullet that was in your shoulder and disinfect the area. All that's left is for me to stitch your wound," Jim said, grabbing a needle and thread.

As Jim began stitching Connor's shoulder, Connor wondered about who the old friend Jim was talking about. *Could they be the ones who killed all the police officers at the hotel? If they are... Where did Jim meet this guy?* Just as Connor was about to ask Jim about their friend, he suddenly received a phone call.

Checking to see who was calling, Connor found that it had a number he didn't recognize. Answering the call, he first heard the voice of a woman gasping. And when he listened to the woman talk, the woman's voice sounded familiar. He soon recognized it to be Anna's voice and she sounded like she was out of breath.

"Anna, are you okay? What's happening?" Connor asked.

"Connor... I need your help. Do you remember the address where Madison was sold to? Well, I went there, and I arrived at this mansion that oversees the city. There are these masked people here... They're chasing after me," Anna said, whispering.

"What? A mansion? Anna, who's chasing after you?" Connor asked but got no response.

A minute passed and Connor still didn't hear from Anna. Fearing the worst, he shouted Anna's name into his phone. However, after doing so, he noticed that someone started breathing heavily.

"Anna? Is that you?" Connor asked but could only hear breathing from Anna's side of the phone.

Listening to the breathing, it was clear to Connor that it wasn't Anna. Clenching his jaw, he frowned, realizing what was happening. By taking a breath, he settled down and focused his thoughts.

"I don't know who you are... And I don't know what you aim to achieve. But I swear to God that I will find you."

"… Good luck," said a man's voice, hanging up the call.

Once the call ended, Connor became speechless, contemplating what had just occurred. Taking a moment to think about what he should do; Connor began tapping his fingers while he had his arms crossed. Meanwhile, Jim watched everything unfold and in the corner of his eye, he glanced at the driver's seat of the van.

Just as Jim was about to speak, Connor stood up and exited the van. Upon stepping outside, Connor's leg failed him and caused him to lean against the brick wall. Having gained his focus, he looked around and realized they were in an alleyway.

"Connor! Where are you going?" Jim shouted, as he also stepped outside the van.

"To go and save Anna! I can't abandon her!" Connor replied, now standing on both legs.

"What? But Connor, you barely know that woman! Why would you risk your life to save her?"

"Because she saved me! When I met her, I was about to die, but she risked her life even though she didn't know who I was… Besides, like you said before, we should love our neighbor just as Jesus would."

Hearing Connor's words rendered Jim speechless as he stood gazing at Connor, seeing how determined he was. At this moment, Jim trusted Connor's judgment and took the keys to the car out of his pocket. But before handing them to Connor, Jim gave Connor his trench coat, shirt, and satchel.

When Connor put on his shirt and trench coat, Jim handed him the keys and said, "I want you to make me a promise that you'll come back to me alive… That's all I ask of you."

"You know, instead of a promise… Try and have faith. Because I know God is with me, he's always been with me.

Seeing how much Connor had changed, Jim smiled as a tear came down his face. Once Connor left the alleyway, he found their car parked along the roadside. Before entering the car, he looked back at Jim and nodded at him.

Watching Connor drive away, Jim began tearing up and fell to his knees. Sobbing on the ground, Jim felt a hand on his shoulder. In tears, Jim looked up and said the following.

"Did I make a mistake? Should I have let him go? You of all people should know how dangerous they are… So why, why didn't you stop me?" Jim said as a *hooded man* stood behind him.

Driving, Connor began thinking of possible places to find a mansion that resembled Anna's description. Having no idea where to look, he drove all over the city, and with no luck in his searches, he rethought Anna's description. *A mansion that oversees the entire city… Why does that sound so familiar? Almost like… I've been to a place like that.* At that moment, he recalled the one place that came to mind when thinking about the description.

"No… It can't be. God, please tell me that I'm wrong… It just can't be true," Connor said, realizing a frightful truth.

Each second Connor spent driving; all he could think about was the potential horror that awaited him. Drawing near where his suspicions lurked, he thought back to the first time he was there. He felt as if he were living a nightmare when he finally arrived at Sterling's manor.

Glancing at the manor's driveway, he saw several extravagant vehicles parked. He also saw a limousine parked that appeared to be the one that he saw Nancy get into. Parking in the manor's driveway, he looked ahead and saw a suit-clad man standing guard at the manor's front door. Upon closer inspection, he noticed that the man wore a mask. The man's mask was the same as those worn by the masked people he saw in the surveillance footage at Mr. Dixon's casino.

Before exiting the car, Connor searched for his satchel and brought out the mask and cloak he had taken from the mayor's secret safe. His frown deepened when he looked at them, knowing what he had to do. Throwing on the black cloak, he finally donned the mask.

Stepping out of the car, Connor, now wearing the cloak and mask, walked up to the manor's front door. Upon walking up to the front door, he'd be confronted by the masked man.

"May I have the password, sir?" the masked man asked, blocking the entrance to the manor.

"Password? Ah, yes of course," Connor responded.

Contemplating what the password might be, Connor reflected on all his evidence. His mind began recollecting everything he found in the mayor's office and Briana's apartment. It was only when he recalled what The Mortem had written in his journal and thought of a possible response.

"… Ave bestia," Connor said, hoping he figured it out.

"… Thank you, sir. Enjoy the reception," said the masked man, opening the front door for Connor.

Entering the manor, Connor walked down a hallway where he felt like he was walking to his death. As he approached the end of the hallway, he began to hear some sort of prayer being chanted. Once he reached the end, another masked man greeted him, opening another door.

"This way, sir," the other masked man said, leading the way.

Following the masked man, Connor's eyes widened when his hunch turned out to be true. He found himself at Sterling's entrance hall, where Sterling's party took place. However, unlike before, the entrance hall was occupied by a crowd of masked people, all wearing the same black cloaks and white masks.

The sight left Connor speechless, and as he looked around, seeing everyone on the floor kneeling. He also noticed that they were chanting a prayer in a language he couldn't understand. To avoid being caught, he also kneeled but didn't chant the prayer.

After chanting for a few minutes, the crowd of masked people stopped when a man in a white cloak walked down the stairs. Taking a closer look, Connor noticed that the man wore a golden version of the mask everyone was wearing. Once the room fell silent, the golden-masked man formed a triangle-shaped hand sign. The rest of the masked people followed the golden-masked man and formed the hand sign.

Following that, the golden-masked man entered the crowd of masked people who began encircling the golden-masked man. In front of the masked crowd, the golden-masked man pulled out a golden dagger from his cloak and began displaying it. The masked crowd was in awe as they held out their hands, praising the golden-masked man. Silence then fell over the crowd, once the golden-masked man made the hush sign.

"We shall now thank our lord for the blessings we have been bestowed. Our money, fame, power… and eternal life. None of it would be possible if not for our great lord. But our gifts aren't free since our great lord still demands something in return. And thanks to our lord, he has already delivered us that which he craves… A sacrifice!" the golden-masked man shouted as the masked crowd cheered.

Having no idea what was about to happen, Connor looked around until he saw two masked men dragging Anna. Seeing Anna blindfolded and bound caused him to frown, glaring at the sight. Clenching his fists, he breathed heavily, thinking of what he could do to save Anna.

He realized that if he did anything that interrupted the sacrifice, it could risk Anna and his own life. As he watched the golden-masked man remove Anna's blindfold, the golden-masked man grabbed hold of her right arm and sliced it with a golden dagger, causing her to start bleeding. Drenching his hand in Anna's blood, the golden-masked man began drawing on the floor. Once the golden-masked man finished, Connor saw that he had drawn a pentagram with Anna's blood.

The sight instantly reminded Connor of the cabin where Jim and he found Billy and when they found Briana inside a pentagram also drawn in blood. Knowing what was about to take place, he knew that he had to act fast. However, as much as he wanted to save Anna, he couldn't do anything but watch.

Proceeding with the ritual, the golden-masked man drew The Star of David on Anna's forehead with her blood. After that, the golden-masked man took out a match and started lighting the candles that other masked people placed down encircling the pentagram. Now dragging Anna inside the pentagram, the golden-masked man gripped onto the golden dagger he carried.

While this was all happening, Connor noticed that Anna wasn't reacting to anything. Assuming they drugged her, he realized it was all up to him. Not knowing what to do, he started praying the lord's prayer under his breath.

"God, please help me… I don't know what to do. I need… a miracle," Connor whispered to himself as tears came down his face.

In the moments before the golden masked man was about to stab Anna, Connor was about to jump in until suddenly a gunshot was heard. As a result, panic ensued in the masked crowd, causing the golden-masked man to stop the sacrifice. The golden-masked man attempted to quiet down the masked crowd, leaving Anna inside the pentagram.

"Everyone settle down! There is no need to panic. We are safe here," said the golden-masked man.

"How do you know for sure? What if it's The Mortem? What if he has found us!" one of the masked people in the crowd shouted.

"We no longer have reason to fear The Mortem anymore… I know this because by now he must be mourning the death of his dear—" the golden masked man said but noticed that two of the masked men that were holding Anna in place had been knocked out.

The golden-masked man looked ahead and saw Connor carrying Anna in his arms. When Connor and the golden-masked man locked eyes, Connor stood there contemplating his next move. With Anna still in his arms, Connor looked around for where he should run and noticed the stairs that led to the second floor. Thus, Connor ran up the stairs, all while carrying Anna. In response, many of the masked people chased after Connor and Anna, but the golden-masked man blocked their way and said the following.

"No, I will pursue them… The rest of you investigate the origin of the gunshot that was heard. Remember, we are the ones who control this world!"

On the second floor, Connor, still holding Anna, looked for a place where they could hide. He came across multiple doors and contemplated which room they should hide in. Knowing time was running out, he chose the nearest one.

Entering the room, he discovered it was the master bedroom, and in the middle of the room was a queen-size bed. Laying Anna on the bed, he then ripped a piece from his cloak and wrapped Anna's bleeding arm. Once he finished wrapping Anna's arm, he cleaned off The Star of David on her forehead and then sat down on a chair nearby. A few minutes passed until he heard Anna waking up. Taking off his mask, he rushed to Anna and stood beside her.

"Anna, wake up. Please, Anna, wake up. I need you to be awake," Connor said, holding Anna's hand.

"Huh? Connor, is that you? You came for me... I can't believe you actually came for me," Anna said as tears came flowing down her face and proceeded to hug Connor.

"What, you thought I was gonna abandon you? No, that's not who I am."

"Yeah, I just realized that... Umm, why does my arm hurt?" Anna said as she looked at her bandaged arm.

"Sorry, I did my best to patch your arm up. But besides that, you're mostly fine," Connor said.

"Heh, well, it's not every day I wake up with a bleeding arm... Umm, Connor, where are we?" Anna said, getting up from the bed.

"We're in one of Sterling's bedrooms... I'm sorry but I couldn't reach the exit since I was surrounded. So, I had to think fast and ran upstairs while I carried you in my arms."

"No, it's fine, don't apologize. You saved me, that's all that matters, and thank you for that... Wait, Sterling? You know the name of the mansion's owner?"

"It's... a long story. I'll explain everything to you once we escape—" Connor said but heard footsteps coming from outside the bedroom.

Listening to the footsteps, both Connor and Anna tried to remain silent. At that moment, Connor felt compelled to act. As a result, he attempted to open the door, but Anna grabbed his arm and pulled him back.

"Are you crazy? What do you think you're doing?" Anna whispered, holding onto Connor's arm.

"We can't stay here for much longer... If we do, we're going to eventually be caught," Connor replied.

"Then what can we do? Unless we jump out of the window, there's nowhere we can run to."

"Hmm, okay you stay here, and I'll go out to distract whoever's out there. And when I have them distracted, you run. Don't worry about me, I'll be fine," Connor said, putting his mask back on.

Opening the door, Connor looked around and saw the golden-masked man checking each door of the hallway. Inspecting the area, he noticed a table nearby. He also saw an owl statue on the table that looked like a possible weapon he could use. Seeing this, he shut the door behind him, ran to the table, and hid behind it. However, the golden-masked man heard him closing the door, causing the golden-masked man to turn around. Beginning to close in on the door where Anna was, the golden-masked man reached out his hand and was about to open the door.

However, Connor jumped out and shouted, "Hey!"

"You... Where is the woman?" the golden-masked man said, turning around.

"Sorry, pal but you're not laying a finger on her."

"Is that so? We will see about that."

As the golden-masked man approached, Connor grabbed the owl statue and hurled it at him. However, the golden-masked man caught the statue and crushed it with his hand. Seeing this, Connor took two steps back, but shook his head and charged at the golden-masked man anyway. He started throwing a barrage of punches, but the golden-masked man evaded all his attacks. Realizing he couldn't land a single punch; he tried increasing the pace of his punches. Yet, he still couldn't hit the golden-masked man. It eventually led to him falling on the floor after exhausting himself.

Standing back up, Connor tried to throw one more punch, but his eyes widened when his arm was caught. Tossing him against a wall, the golden-masked man chuckled, seeing Connor powerless. Having been thrown at a wall, Connor realized something about the golden-masked man wasn't normal.

"What's the matter? You're tired already? I thought you weren't going to let me lay a finger on that woman," the golden-masked man said, standing before Connor.

"Why... can't I hit you?"

"Hmm, perhaps you're just too slow... Or I'm just too fast," the golden-masked man said, appearing right next to Connor in a blink of an eye.

The golden-masked man then grabbed Connor by the neck and started choking him, all with one arm. As a last resort, Connor tried kicking the golden-masked man. However, the golden-masked man didn't even react to any of his kicks as if he didn't feel any of them.

"You will tell me where you hid the woman. But if you won't tell me, you could just take her place... Connor."

"What? How... do you know?" Connor said, struggling to breathe.

"Who do you think was the one that left the clue to the mayor's safe combination? That's Johnson's mask and cloak you're wearing after all."

As Connor continued to be strangled, Anna ran out of the room and charged at the golden-masked man, stabbing him with a piece of broken wood. This resulted in the golden-masked man crying in pain and causing him to release Connor from his grasp. After that, Anna went to Connor and helped him stand back up.

"What did... you do?" Connor asked, struggling to speak.

"I stabbed him with a piece of wood that I ripped out from a chair nearby. But never mind that, let's get out of here before—" Anna said but got interrupted by Connor.

"No, you go! I'll stay behind and keep him busy while you escape," said Connor.

"What? Connor this guy could kill you! If it weren't for me just now, you'd be dead!"

"You don't understand… Even if we both ran, there's no outrunning him. There's something about him that's… unnatural. He'll catch us before we even know it. Please, go while you can. Everything will be fine because I know God is with me and he's with you too. You just need to have faith, Anna."

"… You better know what you're doing," Anna said as she ran down the stairs.

After Anna left, Connor reflected on whether he had made the right choice. Despite this, he trusted God was with him as he looked behind him and saw the golden-masked man struggling to pull out the piece of wood behind him. It wasn't long before the golden-masked man pulled out the piece of wood.

"Now that was oddly brave of you… Although an admirable act, it won't save you from me," the golden-masked man said, taking out the golden dagger from before.

Meanwhile, as Anna walked down the stairs, she gasped at the sight of the masked crowd. Crouching down, Anna hid behind a wall and began looking around. As she did this, she noticed the masked crowd were arguing.

"I say we all go and check together," said one of the masked people.

"No, then that puts all of us at risk! One will go and see who shot that gun," said another one of the masked people.

"This is ridiculous! Why are we all so afraid? Even if this is The Mortem, why should we fear one man? When we are the ones who run this city, who control this world—" a masked woman said but was shot from behind.

Having been shot, the impact from the gunshot caused the woman's mask to fall to the floor, revealing Nancy behind it. Nancy soon dropped dead on the floor and began to stain the floor with her blood. Following this, a slow march of footsteps echoed from the hallway. With each step growing louder, the masked crowd became speechless. It was only when a mysterious hooded man emerged from the hallway. The hooded man also carried a baseball bat stained with blood and had nails drilled into it.

Inspecting the hooded man, Anna noticed that the man was wearing a full-face helmet. Another thing she noticed was that the hooded man wore some kind of body armor. Having realized what was about to take place, she remained where she was and watched from a distance.

As for the hooded man, he remained silent and gazed at the crowd. Breaking the silence, one of the masked people swung a knife at the hooded man. Yet the masked person was disarmed by the hooded man, who then bent their arm backward, causing the masked person to cry out.

Throwing the masked person on the floor, the hooded man clutched onto his nailed baseball bat. The hooded man started to beat the masked person mercilessly to the point where their body had drenched in their blood. When the hooded man had finished off the masked person, he slowly raised his head and glanced at the rest.

Following this, the masked crowd panicked and searched for an exit. But their efforts were in vain, as the hooded man slaughtered them all. One by one, the hooded man beat, shot, and stabbed all the masked people. But one of the masked people managed to evade the hooded man's carnage and attempted to crawl away. However, the hooded man stepped on their feet, stopping them in their tracks.

"No, please! Spare me! Look, I'm very rich. Is it money you want from us? If so, I could make you a millionaire—" the masked person said but ultimately got shot in the head by the hooded man.

Anna's heart couldn't stop beating, after having witnessed a massacre. Taking a deep breath, she eventually came to her senses again. Rubbing her eyes, she glanced behind the wall, but was was then met by the hooded man.

"I'm not one of them! Please don't kill me," Anna pleaded as she trembled.

The hooded man had Anna at gunpoint and began to inspect Anna for a moment. Eventually, the hooded man lowered his gun and nodded to the hallway. With her heart racing, Anna gradually stood up, and without taking her eyes off the hooded man, she slowly made her way to the hallway. Upon arriving, she ran down the hallway until she reached the front door, where she discovered a masked man dead on the floor. She was then confronted by Jim, who aimed a revolver at her, after opening the front door.

Realizing that Anna wasn't one of the masked people, Jim lowered his revolver and said, "Oh dear, please forgive me. You must be Anna! It's a pleasure to meet you."

"Umm, who are you?" Anna asked.

"Oh, well my name is Jim… I'm Connor's partner."

"Jim? I think Connor mentioned you once."

"Did he? Well, I hope he mentioned good things… Anyway, where is Connor?"

Back on the second floor, Connor and the golden-masked man stood before each other, exchanging glares. Removing the mayor's mask, Connor threw it to the floor. Without taking his eyes off the golden-masked man, Connor inspected the golden-masked man's mask and noticed something familiar. He noticed that the golden-masked man had the same symbol on his mask that Briana had, a star of David with an eye in the center.

"You people control this city, probably even the entire world... Just who are you people anyway?" Connor asked, starting to finally connect the dots.

"Wouldn't you like to know... Heh, very well, I will tell you. We are the ones who pull the strings of every mayor, every politician, every governor, every president, every celebrity, and every police officer. Anyone who is in some sort of position of power, we control them. We... are the order of the Illuminati! And I am The Grand-Master."

"The Illuminati? But that's just a conspiracy theory?"

"And a theory we are... to the public. But only a very few know the truth, and that includes you now. Usually these few are given two choices when they learn the truth. They either join us... or die. That is why I left that clue at the mayor's office in case the chief were to fail in terminating you and your partner, Jim... Please accept my invitation and join us, Connor. I know you have great potential. Just imagine, you could be one of us. All powerful as we worship our great lord!"

"No! I'd never join you, people! Not to mention worshiping a so-called *lord* I don't even recognize as my God!"

"... I'm very disappointed Connor. Not only did you reject my invitation... you've insulted our great lord. For that... you *will* take the place of that woman and I will bury this dagger deep into your beating heart!" The Grand-Master shouted as he bolted toward Connor and left a cut on his arm.

Slashing at Connor, The Grand-Master cut him from left to right, until Connor was covered in gashes. *Is this guy even human? How is he moving so fast?* Trying to fight back, Connor attempted to throw a punch at The Grand-Master, but it got caught again.

Having Connor's arm in his grasp, The Grand-Master looked around and caught a glimpse of the balcony. Connor heard a chuckle from the Grand-Master, who grabbed Connor's shirt and hurled him at the balcony. Because the impact was so great, the patio doors shattered as he landed on the balcony.

As Connor bled on the floor of the balcony, The Grand-Master inhaled and said, "Oh I just *love* the smell of blood... It's intoxicating."

"Wait, before you kill me... Tell me who you are!" Connor shouted, bleeding.

"Oh please, Connor, you should already know the answer to that by now. Just look where we're standing... Tell me, what's my name?"

"... Sterling, your name is Charles Sterling!"

"Well done, you've figured it out... Now, shall we finish our game of chess from before?" Sterling said, taking off his golden mask.

Connor's eyebrows lowered, seeing that the one person he thought remained on his side, ultimately ended up being another lie. Despite his bleeding, Connor managed to stand, holding himself onto the balcony railing. While he held himself up, he felt a pain in his arm and remembered that his arm was still broken.

"… I never wanted it to come to this. The two of us, against one another. This reminds me of when old Dixon tried to oppose us… He learned the hard way after I ordered his father to be killed. But that's the beauty of chess isn't it not?"

"My God, you're insane… Sterling, what you people are doing is evil… Don't you feel any guilt? What about Briana? She did nothing wrong, but you people killed her! Where's your humanity?" Connor asked.

"That woman was used as a sacrifice for our great lord! An appropriate punishment for sticking her nose where she shouldn't… And as for my humanity. I'm afraid I lost that a long time ago."

"What does that mean?"

"Hmm, it'd be better if you don't know… Though, I do believe it's about time we end this," Sterling said, clutching onto the golden dagger.

Cornered on the balcony, there was nowhere Connor could escape. While Sterling approached with his golden dagger in hand, Connor held onto his faith. Just as Sterling was about to stab him, he heard a gun being fired.

With his eyes widened, Sterling glanced behind him and saw the hooded man standing before him. The hooded man proceeded to shoot Sterling several more times, causing Sterling to fall over the rail of the balcony. Gasping at the sight, Connor looked down and saw Sterling land on the driveway of the manor.

Witnessing Sterling's death, Connor turned around and saw the hooded man. Covered in blood, the hooded man proceeded to drop his pistol on the floor. The hooded man then removed his hood, showing a battered full-face helmet. Following the removal of his hood, the man removed his helmet, revealing something Connor never would have expected.

"Hey, brother… You missed me?" the hooded man said, showing his face.

"… Michael?" Connor said, but blacked out, collapsing on the balcony floor.

Epilogue
The Doctor

Inspecting the corpse of Sterling, Jim caught a glimpse of the multiple bullet holes in Sterling's clothing. However, Jim noticed that they didn't have blood coming out from them. Though this appeared strange to Jim, he shrugged it off and then noticed Michael exiting the manor, carrying Connor in his arms.

"Connor! Connor, are you hurt? Talk to me, son!" Jim cried out.

"Is he still… alive?" Anna asked.

"He's alive… But he's lost a lot of blood," Michael replied.

"We need to take him to a hospital!" Jim shouted.

"No! We can't do that. A hospital is the first place they'll look. But don't worry, my van has everything we need to patch him up," Michael replied, placing Connor inside the van.

"God damn it, Michael! I knew it was a mistake to let Connor leave with the car! Why didn't you stop me?"

"… I was afraid alright! I never wanted either of you to be involved in this… I blame myself. They found out who I was and when the chief hired you two, it was their way of sending me a message. I had to completely abandon what I was trying to achieve here… While I did the best I could to keep you and Connor safe!"

"If you really wanted to keep me and Connor safe, why did you have to become this? Why didn't you come back to us? Back to your only brother, who has mourned you? You still haven't explained to me how you're even alive!"

After a few minutes of silence, Jim entered the van and began treating Connor with a first aid kit. Anna stood beside Jim, watching Jim disinfect Connor's gashes. Michael, meanwhile, took out a map of the United States from his leather hoodie.

"Alright, I have a place where we can stay… I own a warehouse in Iowa. We'll be safe there in the meantime," Michael explained, shoving the map back into his hoodie's pocket.

"You own a warehouse? Since when were you able to afford something like that?" Jim asked.

"Best if I explain that later… Anyway, let's get moving before any more Illuminati cunts show up," Michael said, closing the van's doors, but noticed Anna stepping inside the van.

Yanking Anna out of the van, Michael aimed his pistol at Anna, which resulted in Anna shouting, "Hey, the fuck is wrong with you?"

"What's wrong with me? Where do you think you're going? You're not coming with us—" Michael said, but got interrupted by Jim, who exited the van.

"Michael, you leave her alone! She is coming with us… If Connor trusts her, then I trust her."

"… Hmm, fine. But I swear if you hurt my brother or betray us… I'll kill you," Michael said, walking away and entering the van's driver's seat.

Following this, Anna sat next to Connor in the back of the van, while Jim tended to Connor's wounds. At the same time, Michael started the van's engine and drove away. After the four drove off, Sterling's eyes suddenly opened. Shortly after Sterling's awakening, he heard footsteps coming from his manor.

"I'm not surprised that you managed to survive The Mortem's wrath… Nancy," Sterling said, brushing some dirt off his cloak.

"Ditto… But then again, it would have been nice not having to feel the pain of getting shot. Which is a privilege you get to have my *dear* Grand Master," Nancy said, taking out the bullet from her back.

"I never thought I'd hear some jealousy from you my dear… Nancy, you will want to keep quiet because… the master has arrived."

After arriving at his manor's driveway, a limousine pulled up. Once the limousine parked, a masked man in a suit stepped out of the driver's door. Exiting the limousine, a man dressed as a plague doctor stepped out, carrying a staff. The two then bowed down before the plague doctor.

"Forgive me, master… But tonight's ritual was ruined along with my failure in *breaking* The Mortem. I did everything you asked, and I even ordered the chief to kill The Mortem's brother and the brother's partner…. But the chief failed and as a result, I failed you," said Sterling.

"Not to worry, you said the chief failed… So, the blame lies on the chief. I've also been recently informed that the chief was found dead at a construction site… with a pistol in his hand. He didn't break his oath, so his mother won't be killed."

"I see… But master, we might not have been able to break The Mortem, but something I've just learned may prove useful."

"Did you? Well, you can tell me on the way… Oh, and I should have mentioned this before, but I prefer to be simply called *The Doctor*."

To Be Continued...

THE AUTHOR

Photo by: Dahiana Merlina

Author's Note

The story I had for this book has changed a lot over the past few years. In the end, I came up with this story as the start of a saga I hope to complete someday. Anyway, if all goes well, I'll be able to make a sequel to this novel soon. Oh, and yes, every illustration, including the cover, was done by me. Lastly, I want to thank my mom, Dahiana, for never giving up on me and for being there for me every step of the way when making this novel.

NANDO.WRITES